"Really, Ted, you could end up driving around for fifteen minutes. I don't need to be walked to the door."

This wasn't a real date, anyway, Sara Beth reminded herself.

"Thank you for going with me tonight." He reached over and pressed her shoulder, his fingertips grazing her neck.

Her breath caught. The air around her crackled. Neither of them moved. She wanted to kiss him, and she saw his gaze drop to her mouth and linger, his fingers twitching at the same time, then digging in a little.

Move, she ordered herself. Get out. Don't look back.

She didn't budge.

Dear Reader,

One of life's biggest heartbreaks can be someone's inability to conceive a child. Doctors and researchers have worked tirelessly to change that painful situation, with increasing success. My hero, Ted Bonner, is such a doctor, a man on a mission to treat infertility. I imagine him to be like so many others in that field: dedicated, devoted and driven.

But Ted needs balance in his life, too. So along comes nurse Sara Beth O'Connell, a woman just as dedicated to her work, but one who also knows how to relax—and to love. She has a lot to teach Dr. Bonner.

I had a great time playing in the same sandbox with the other terrific and talented authors in this series. I hope you enjoy the results of the fun we all had.

All my best,

Susan

THE DOCTOR'S PREGNANT BRIDE?

SUSAN CROSBY

Silhouette®

SPECIAL EDITION®

Published by Silhouette Books

America's Publisher of Contemporary Romance

Special thanks and acknowledgment to Susan Crosby
for her contribution to The Baby Chase miniseries.

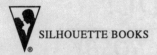 **SILHOUETTE BOOKS**

ISBN-13: 978-0-373-65512-0

THE DOCTOR'S PREGNANT BRIDE?

Recycling programs
for this product may
not exist in your area.

Visit Silhouette Books at www.eHarlequin.com

Printed in U.S.A.

Books by Susan Crosby

SUSAN CROSBY

believes in the value of setting goals, but also in the magic of making wishes, which often do come true—as long as she works hard enough. Along life's journey she's done a lot of the usual things—married, had children, attended college a little later than the average coed and earned a B.A. in English. Then she dove off the deep end into a full-time writing career, a wish come true.

Susan enjoys writing about people who take a chance on love, sometimes against all odds. She loves warm, strong heroes and good-hearted, self-reliant heroines, and she will always believe in happily ever after.

More can be learned about her at www.susancrosby.com.

To Paul, aka "Fandango," fellow foodie,
with great appreciation—for your indefatigable help
with research, legal and otherwise, and for all the times
you crack me up. Thank you.

Chapter One

Sara Beth O'Connell slowed her bike to a stop at a red light, her gaze fixed on it. Red, the color of hearts and roses—

A car honked, jolting her into action. She pedaled through the intersection, picking up the bike lane again on the other side. The air was unusually mild and the traffic Sunday-afternoon light in Cambridge, Massachusetts, giving her time to think, time to decide that she wasn't really bothered by not having a date on Valentine's Day. It was more about what being dateless implied—that there was no one special enough in her life to spend the romantic evening with.

So what, right? No big deal. Only the minute hand on her biological clock was ticking, not the hour hand.

And then there was the man in the grocery store earlier…

Sara Beth tossed her head, her bike helmet preventing her long hair from falling into her face as she rode into the employee parking lot of the Armstrong Fertility Institute, the understated but modern structure where she worked as head nurse. Eyeing Lisa Armstrong's car in the distance, she locked her bike to a rack, then moved to the employee entrance. She slid her ID card into the security reader and pressed her thumb against a pad until a buzzer went off, unlocking the door.

Once inside, her footsteps barely registered in the quiet building as she headed to Lisa's office, finding her door open. The head administrator of the institute, a research center and fertility clinic, sat in front of her computer, her slender frame hunched, her dark eyes focused on the screen.

Sara Beth drew a calming breath, not because she was annoyed that Lisa had called her into the office on a Sunday, but because of the memory of the man Sara Beth had seen that morning buying a stuffed teddy and gummy bears for his five-year-old daughter. *My Valentine,* he'd called her when the clerk commented on the items. Sara Beth hadn't been lucky enough to have a father do that for her. This morning's reminder of that loss curled painfully inside her.

Ignoring the flash of pain, she set her helmet on top of a file cabinet, unzipped her jacket then plopped into a chair on the other side of Lisa's desk. "What's so all-fired important that it couldn't wait until tomorrow? Or you couldn't tell me on the phone?"

Lisa blinked. "You have something better to do?"

"Just because you work 24/7 doesn't mean I have to, you know," Sara Beth said, not letting Lisa off easy. "It *is* Valentine's Day."

Lisa's smile was a little crooked. Her dark eyes shimmered knowingly. "You don't have a date."

"How do you know?"

"How long have we been best friends, Sara Beth?"

Sarah Beth pulled off her jacket, not wanting to make eye contact, not wanting Lisa to play the best-friends card for whatever it was she'd called Sara Beth in on a Sunday for. "Since before we spoke our first words."

"Twenty-eight years. If you had a date tonight, I would know." Lisa sat back, looking satisfied with herself. "You tell me everything."

"Not everything."

"Everything important."

Sara Beth sniffed. "A date on Valentine's Day isn't important."

Lisa laughed.

After a moment, Sara Beth smiled. "So, what's up? Why the command performance?"

Lisa lowered her voice. "Shut the door, please."

"Someone else is in the building?" Sara Beth asked, complying. "Someone else doesn't know that weekends are for relaxation?"

"As a matter of fact—Dr. Bonner."

Which meant he didn't have a date, either. If a man

like Ted Bonner didn't have a date, she couldn't feel sorry for herself. Except, he still could have dinner plans. It wasn't too late for that. She wouldn't have minded going out with him herself....

"This has something to do with Dr. Bonner?" Sara Beth asked.

"Everything to do with him. You know the investigation he's supposed to be running on the protocol errors he and Dr. Demetrios discovered right after we hired them a few months back?"

"Of course."

"They haven't come up with results yet. We've learned that some outsiders are starting to question our recent cluster of multiple births. Bad press will hurt us, especially our funding. We already narrowly escaped a disaster when that magazine article was published a while back about donor eggs being misused here. We can't afford another problem, or even a hint of one. We need answers, Sara Beth, before the press gets wind of this one."

"Not just answers but exoneration," Sara Beth said.

"Well, yes, of course, but first and foremost, we need to know whether information has been falsified or breached in the past—or whatever the truth is. And we need to know now."

"How does that affect me?"

Lisa leaned her elbows on her desk. "We want you to assist Drs. Bonner and Demetrios so that the project gets done. You will report to us if they're doing anything to stall the investigation."

She would be working directly for the man she'd had a serious lust for since she'd first laid eyes on him?

"Um, us?" she asked.

"Paul and me."

"Why would the doctors stall? They weren't part of the problem, if there is a problem. It happened before they were hired."

"Because even a whisper of scandal could affect donations and grant money, which will limit Dr. Bonner's and Dr. Demetrios's hope of success in their research—not to mention the institute's reputation and credibility. If something unethical has been going on, our funds could dry up and their jobs could be eliminated. Wouldn't you stall if that was about to happen to you?"

Sara Beth didn't believe she would, but that was her.

"So you're asking me to spy on them?"

"I wouldn't call it that. We're just lighting a fire under the doctors to get action before we get burned on this. You love the institute, and my father. This has to be important to you."

"Absolutely." The institute, and especially its founder, Dr. Gerald Armstrong, had been very generous to Sara Beth's mother so that she could retire early and comfortably. He'd been good to Sara Beth, as well.

"You're loyal to me, too," Lisa said.

"It goes without saying. Not just you, but also your brother Paul as chief of staff. But you know how I feel about deceit." Most of her life Sara Beth had been haunted by not knowing who her father was, which felt like an enormous deceit to her. All she knew was he'd been a sperm donor here at the fertility institute founded by Lisa's father, whom Sara Beth affectionately called Dr. G.

Anonymous donors never brought teddy bears or candy on Valentine's Day. Or sent birthday cards. Or pretended to be Santa. Or tucked a tired little girl in bed at night. Only a father did that.

"I do know how you feel about deceit," Lisa said. "That's my point. You could be *uncovering* a lie. Isn't that reason enough?"

Sara Beth wandered to the window but didn't really take in the sights. Could she pull it off?

Lisa joined her. "You're the eyes and ears of the institute, because in your job capacity you bridge both aspects of what we do, the medical *and* the research programs. You haven't hesitated to tell me when you've noticed something needing looking into, so how is this any different? Except that this time you're being assigned to observe and report something specific. Otherwise it's business as usual."

Lisa had a point. "What if they don't want me on board?"

"They won't have a choice."

"But how effective can I be if they won't cooperate?"

"When did you become such a worrier?" Lisa cocked her head. "You've always been optimistic and adventurous. What's going on?"

Sara Beth couldn't share what was going on, not this time, because she wasn't sure herself, except that lately, and especially today, she'd been feeling a little lost. Left out.

Lonely. She was missing a father she'd never known, and wishing for a man in her life, as well, a man to love and cherish, and be a hands-on father to whatever children they were blessed with.

She loved her job, but she didn't want to end up like her mother, who'd never married, having been married to the institute. And yet Sara Beth could see that she was following in her mother's footsteps, even taking on the job of head nurse, like her mom. Where *had* Sara Beth's adventurousness gone?

Being asked to spy for the good of the institute would be an adventure of sorts, wouldn't it? More important, their work was critical to the many people whose deepest dreams they helped fulfill—having a child.

"All right. I'll do it."

"Thank you." Relief coated Lisa's quiet words. "Let's go talk to Dr. Bonner."

Sara Beth clamped her mouth against the "Now?" that threatened to come out. She wanted to face him in her official capacity, wearing her uniform, her scrubs. Instead she wore cycling pants, a Boston College T-shirt and her old, comfortable riding sneakers. She'd left her hair down instead of pulled away from her face as usual, out of her way, her helmet taking care of that problem.

It wasn't the best way to start their new association, not as far as she was concerned, not if she wanted to keep a professional relationship—which she did. Unfortunately.

Sara Beth walked silently beside Lisa as they made their way through the cavernous hallways of the building, past the administration section, past examination rooms and consultation areas. During the workweek the hallways were alive with people. It wasn't a boisterous place—the work they did was too important to be treated frivolously—but it was always pleasant, the employees chosen not only for their abilities but their personalities. No drama allowed.

Until now, she'd only seen Dr. Bonner in passing or through the windows of the lab where he did his research. His partner, Chance Demetrios, was much more social and talkative, plus he was also a practicing physician, not just a researcher. Sara Beth often assisted him in his ob-gyn practice, whereas Dr. Ted Bonner had apparently discovered that he was better suited to the lab than patients. His too-direct bedside manner evidently wasn't the best for inspiring confidence or easing anyone's fears.

At least, that was the rumor floating around about him. Since she'd rarely had a discussion with him longer than "Nice to meet you" or "Good morning," she couldn't verify anything else. She'd intentionally avoided conversations with him because her throat closed when she was around him, something that never happened with anyone else. She always wanted to comb his hair away from his forehead with her fingers, too.

When Sara Beth and Lisa reached the lab, they stood side by side peering through the glass at the man inside. Tall, dark and gorgeous was a cliché, but the description fit him, if in an intellectual way. His hair brushed his neck, but she figured he'd just forgotten to get a haircut lately. Every so often he got it cut, and when he did, it was very short, as if he couldn't be bothered with regular trims.

He truly fit the stereotype of the absentminded professor: black-framed glasses; long white lab coat, pocket protector and all, his personal uniform; along with a white or blue dress shirt and dark slacks.

She shouldn't find him sexy, but she did. She'd heard he often forgot to eat, which was probably why he was so lean and wiry, and which also made him look even taller than his well-over-six-foot frame.

Lisa knocked. He continued entering information into a computer, his fingers flying over the keyboard. She knocked again. Still no response. Sara Beth looked to see if he was wearing earbuds and listening to music. He was only thirty-two, of an age to blast tunes in his head and work at the same time. No earbuds were visible, no dangling cords, either.

"Let's just wait until tomorrow," Sara Beth said, tugging on Lisa's arm. "He's in some impenetrable zone, that's for sure."

"I wonder if a fire alarm would get his attention?"

Sara Beth stared at her friend. "You wouldn't—"

"Of course not." Lisa laughed. "I was thinking out loud. You know, what would happen if? Would he hear it in time to escape?"

"He can't be *that* bad. Come on. Let's just go. He's doing important work, and we shouldn't disturb—"

Lisa entered her security information, turned the doorknob and stepped inside. Sara Beth sighed and followed.

"Good afternoon, Dr. Bonner," Lisa said as she drew close.

He didn't startle, but Sara Beth saw awareness click in. For one thing, he blinked. He held up a hand briefly then continued to type.

Sara Beth glanced around the lab. The two waist-high lab tables were neat and orderly, even loaded with equipment as they were—microscopes with projection screens, computers, other high-tech pieces she couldn't identify. Then there was the low-tech, standard lab equipment—stainless-steel sinks, glass vessels and tubes. Everything seemed to have its place, all order, no chaos.

Why aren't you on a date tonight, Dr. Gorgeous? she wondered. He was young, handsome and gainfully employed. She'd always assumed he played the field as much as his inveterate-flirt research partner, Dr. Demetrios, did.

"Ms. Armstrong," he said finally, turning toward Lisa. "And Ms. O'Connell. What can I do for you?" His gaze zeroed in and held on Sara Beth in an unnerving way as he gave her the same kind of complete attention he had given the computer just moments ago.

Not a multitasker, she decided, fascinated, as he took off his glasses and set them on the tabletop then shoved his fingers through his rich brown hair. She itched to do the same.

"I know you've been frustrated, Dr. Bonner," Lisa said, "at being unable to find answers to the protocol problems."

"An understatement."

"Well, I've brought the cavalry." Lisa turned toward

Sara Beth. "We've decided to free up Sara Beth from some of her regular assignments and let her help you and Dr. Demetrios with your investigation."

For a few long moments he stayed silent, his expression giving away nothing, then he said, "Her help is gratefully accepted."

That was way too easy, Sara Beth thought. Which was a good thing, right? If they could work without dissension, they could cover a lot more ground more quickly. Maybe she wouldn't feel as if she was spying, either. And maybe her pulse would stop pounding so hard.

"On one condition," he added. "Call me Ted. You, too, Sara Beth."

Sara Beth waited for Lisa's reply. Lisa's father, the institute's founder, had always insisted on using titles. But then, not only was he retired, he was almost completely bedridden. He never came into the institute anymore.

Lisa's shoulders relaxed. "Except in front of patients or VIPs."

"Fair enough."

"Should I call Dr. Demetrios or would you like to tell him?"

Ted pulled a cell phone from his pocket and pushed one button, then waited. "I hope I'm not disturbing you, Chance." His brows went up at whatever Dr. Demetrios's response was. "I'll make it quick, then. I just wanted you to know that Ms. O'Connell will be assisting us for a while so that we can get to the bottom of the issues around here…. Yes, Sara Beth…. Yes, the one with the long, dark red hair. How many other Ms. O'Connells are there? You work with her every— Oh. A joke."

He tipped the phone down. "When are you starting?"

"Immediately," Lisa answered.

Pride made Sara Beth not want him to know she didn't have a date for Valentine's Day, so she started to say she would start the next day, but he spoke first.

"Is tomorrow okay?" he asked Sara Beth. "I have plans tonight."

So. He *did* have a date. "That'd be fine."

"Tomorrow," Dr. Bonner said into the phone. "Yes, I'll do that. Bye."

He slid his phone back into his pocket. "Chance extends his thanks."

"I'll leave you two to work out a schedule." Lisa headed toward the door. "Sara Beth, you can plan on giving ten to fifteen hours a week to the project."

Then she was gone, and Sara Beth was left with Dr. Bon—Ted. Without Lisa as a buffer, they would have to talk....

"I'm looking forward to working with you," she said, twining her fingers. "I hope I can help you find the answers you need."

"Me, too. It's been frustrating. I'm a scientist. Discovering the truth is what I do."

The way he said that made him seem like a superhero, a man whose ethical core was the heart and soul of him, as if truth mattered more than anything in the world.

"What can I do?" she asked.

"Nothing that you'll find exciting. In fact, it's tedious

and painstaking, but it's the only way to get the answers. We need to know if previous doctors implanted too many embryos or manipulated the statistics to boost the institute's success numbers and therefore increase funding. So far we've been working with our more recent computerized records, but in order to dispute some of the claims, you might spend time reading old files from the archives vault, cross-checking and rechecking test results from before the institute switched to the new computer system."

The archive vault? Whatever else he said was lost. The archive vault. *The* vault. She would have reason to go inside it.

Her heart thundered, a deafening pounding in her chest. What had been denied her all her life was within her reach—because in the vault was her mother's medical file, detailing her artificial insemination.

A hundred times Sara Beth had almost asked Lisa to help her find that file, and a hundred times she'd decided not to risk their friendship by asking. Lisa never could have allowed it, even for her very best friend.

And now, if Sara Beth was lucky, she could find a reference to the name of the man who'd donated the sperm that had given her life.

Forget paper hearts. This could be her red-letter day.

Chapter Two

Ted stopped talking when he saw Sara Beth tune out, something that usually only happened to him when he was explaining data or experiment results, which wasn't the case this time. He'd only been telling her what tasks in the investigation she could take on in order to speed things up.

She was looking straight at him, her dark brown eyes glazed over. Should he wait for her to refocus or try to snap her out of it?

He decided to give her a moment, noting that she looked different today. Younger…

Her hair was down and loose—that was it. She usually had it pulled back in a braid as no-nonsense as her personality. Not that she was cold, but professional. Always. At least with him. He'd perceived her as shy at first, then had seen her interact with others and was bewildered by how she always seemed to avoid him.

She'd caught his eye, of course, during the months he'd been working at the institute, but he'd seen what could happen when coworkers got involved romantically, so he'd avoided even engaging her in conversation, taking away any possibility of temptation at all.

When he and Chance had accepted the offer to come to Cambridge to continue their research, he'd vowed to himself that he would try to be more aware of the world around him, to be more social, but that plan had been foiled almost immediately. He'd questioned the institute's various protocols, finding some statistics that didn't seem feasible, exaggerating the institute's success rate. Although he and Chance hadn't been involved in or responsible for the questionable issues, it was up to them to find the answers.

For Ted, work was all consuming. His research to find a reliable way to treat male infertility took precedence, but clearing up the protocol issues came a close second. As for a personal life, he didn't have one, and couldn't figure out how Chance managed to have his practice, do research and still have time to date. Ted couldn't manage all that.

He finally waved a hand in front of Sara Beth's face.

She jerked back slightly, her cheeks brightening. "Oh, I'm so sorry. I don't know where I went. You were saying?"

"You wanted to know what your duties would entail. I spelled them out."

"Specifically what will I be looking for?"

He gestured her toward a tall lab chair, then sat in the one beside it. "Do you know what I found? What I'm trying to verify?"

"I'd like to hear your take on it."

He got distracted by her sneakers, which she propped on the bottom rung, their scuffed toes at odds with her usually impeccable appearance. "You graduated from BC?" he asked, glancing at her T-shirt imprinted with the Boston College's flying eagle mascot, Baldwin.

She frowned at the change of subject. "From the Connell School of Nursing, yes. The institute gave me a full scholarship."

"I would venture to say you *earned* a full scholarship."

She seemed to relax for the first time since she'd walked into the lab. "I always loved to study."

"Me, too. I still do."

She gave him a knowing smile, as if he'd stated the obvious, which he supposed he had. He much preferred the confines of his lab to dealing with patients on a daily basis. He hated imparting bad news. And in the infertility business, bad news came frequently. He was happier in the lab.

"So, you were going to tell me about what you found," Sara Beth prompted.

"Shortly after Chance and I came on board here, we discovered that some of the lab's protocols weren't measuring up. Data was incomplete or missing. Statistics weren't matching results. Just as we were digging into the problems, *Keeping Up with Medicine* ran that story alleging that donor eggs and sperm had been switched for some clients, which raised all sorts of ethical questions about how we do business."

"The article never named the source of the allegations."

"Nor confirmed them. Then they were proved unfounded and a retraction was made. But at the same time that we were working on that issue, we discovered an out-of-the-ordinary number of multiple births following in vitro over the past few years."

"Which means what?"

"Numbers that big could pad the institute's statistics, making the program seem more successful than it is. We have standards about how many embryos to implant. It looks like the standards might have been ignored. Because of the unusual success rate, the institute was able to obtain a lot more private donations and grant money than usual. Now the numbers are being challenged, and rightfully so."

What he wasn't telling her was that every step he'd taken to resolve the problems had been met with resistance by Derek Armstrong, Paul and Lisa's brother and the institute's CFO. Chance was the only person Ted had confided in about *that*—so far. He couldn't make accusations without proof, but Ted suspected Derek was involved somehow, whether as part of a cover-up or something even worse.

"So, first of all," Ted continued, "we need to prove or disprove the statistics. Then we need to create a best-practices manual of lab protocols, so if we're ever questioned again, the answers will be readily available and backed up. I can use all the help I can get. The institute's reputation is on the line, but so is my ability to continue my research."

She rubbed her hands together, as if anxious to get started right away. "I'll check the appointment schedule for the rest of the week and see what I can do to re-arrange things and free myself up. Would you prefer morning or afternoon?"

"First thing in the morning."

She climbed off the chair and stuck out her hand. "Then I'll see you tomorrow."

He stayed seated, keeping himself closer to eye level. Her hand felt small in his, and warm, but also firm and direct. One of the traits he valued most in people was competency. She hadn't been promoted to head nurse without proving her competency. "I'm looking forward to working with you, Sara Beth."

"Thank you. I feel the same."

He believed it. Her expression showed anticipa-tion, as if she really couldn't wait to get started. He'd tried to get across to her how tedious the work would be, especially if she had to work with the old files in the vault, poring over the folders. Well, she'd find out soon enough.

"Have a nice evening," he said.

"You, too." She headed toward the door, then turned around, walking backward. "Happy Valentine's Day."

Valentine's— Damn. "Oh, uh, same to you," he said, but the door had already closed behind her.

Damn. Once again he'd screwed up. He glanced at his watch. He'd intended to leave more than an hour ago to buy a gift. Aside from the traditional, uncreative grocery-store offerings, what could he buy? When he'd lived in San Francisco he'd gotten away with having something sent, but Boston was home. He didn't have that excuse anymore. He needed to take a personal gift this time, something thoughtful.

From the lab window he spotted Lisa outside standing next to Sara Beth, hugging her helmet and laughing, looking much more carefree than the Sara Beth who'd just left his lab.

He went still. Thoughts swirled. A plan formed. She might be of some help....

Ted locked his computer, tossed his lab coat toward a hook, then raced out of the building as Lisa drove off. He encountered Sara Beth as she was buckling her helmet. Her face registered surprise—and a little wariness—as he descended on her.

"I know we barely know each other," he said. "But hear me out, please."

"Okay." The word came out slowly, curiously.

"This is the first time I've been home for Valentine's Day since I graduated from high school."

"Boston is home?"

He just nodded. "I'm supposed to be at my parents' house in forty-five minutes for dinner. I need to take a gift."

"I'm sure you'll be able to find roses at almost any market."

"And my mother would say 'how lovely' and that would be that. I want to do better than that. I want *you* to be my parents' gift."

Her big brown eyes opened wide. "Excuse me?"

He was pretty sure if she hadn't been straddling her bike, she would've taken a few steps back, deciding he was a mad scientist.

"If they think I'm dating someone, it'll make them happier than anything I could buy." He stopped short of begging, but appealed to the female tendency to nurture. "I know I'm asking an enormous favor. I know there's no reason for you to say yes. You may—you probably *do* have a date already."

Of course she would have plans, an attractive woman like her. He felt ridiculous now for asking.

"There's not enough time," she said finally, gesturing to her bike. "I would have to ride home and get myself ready."

"We're not formal. I'm wearing what I have on, just adding a sport coat."

She gave him a skeptical look.

He nodded toward his car. "I've got a bike rack."

Fifteen minutes later he pulled up in front of her beautiful old Victorian house, said he'd find a place to park, then come back with her bike, giving her no more time to answer than he had in the parking lot, not allowing her any opportunity to say no.

He understood now the expression about someone having a deer-in-the-headlights look. She mumbled something about how to get to her second-floor apartment, then headed toward the house.

He got lucky, coming across a car leaving just a block away. He hauled her bike to her place, where the front door was ajar. He climbed the stairs inside to her unit, where her door hung open.

"Where do you want this?" he asked, rolling her bike inside.

She pointed to an empty spot in the living room. "I'll hurry."

She rushed into a room down the hallway, shutting the door behind her.

Ted glanced around her living room. The house was probably built around the turn of the twentieth century, but had been remodeled recently, although still using original-looking hardwood floors, and an up-to-date kitchen with stainless-steel appliances. And yet the combined living room/dining area/kitchen space was also feminine. Flowers and pottery and bright colors and…comfort. Her furniture was built for sinking into, and looked inviting.

One of these days he would get around to buying his own sofa.

She had a nice view of the street. Most of the houses were from the same era, some better taken care of than others. She lived only blocks from the Red Line. She could take the subway or a bus to work, the bus being more practical—

What if he factored in twice as much of the primary enzyme…?

Ted grabbed a piece of paper and pen from her kitchen counter, sat down and started making notes, getting lost in a possibility he hadn't considered before. Later—and he had no idea how much later—he felt a tap on his shoulder.

He lifted his head so sharply he knocked into her. She yelped, fell back, grabbed her chin. He caught her by the arm to keep her from falling, the back of his hand accidentally pressing into her breast, her firm breast, surprisingly full for such a petite woman.

He let go. She steadied herself, repeatedly rubbing her chin, her cheeks flushing a little, too.

"I apologize, Sara Beth." He gestured toward the three pieces of paper he'd been using to capture his thoughts. "I didn't hear you. Are you all right? May I take a look?"

"I'm sure I'll be fine."

"I am a doctor, you know."

"And I know nothing about medicine?"

He smiled at the teasing tone in her voice, ran his thumb over her chin. "Move your jaw." Her lemon-scented perfume made his nose twitch and drew him closer. "Everything feel normal?"

"I'm fine. Really." She stepped back, and he finally got a full picture of her. Basic black dress, with long sleeves, the neckline not too low or too high, a gold locket, her hair down and curled, high heels that gave her a few inches extra height, which was probably why he'd banged directly into her chin.

"You look nice," he said, an understatement.

"Thank you." She frowned slightly. "Are you sure we can pull this off? It's kind of hard to pretend we've been dating when we really don't know anything about each other."

"We can exchange bios during the drive. If we say

we've only recently started dating, they won't expect us to know everything about each other."

"Well, that much is the truth, anyway." She grabbed her evening bag and keys. "It should be an adventure."

"You think so?"

She nodded. "And *adventure* is my middle name."

He couldn't tell if she was serious or joking, then her eyes twinkled mischievously, and he found that appealing. He tended to date serious women—

Whoa. Wait. This wasn't a *date* date. This was a please-rescue-me date. No kiss good-night at the door. No how-long-should-I-wait-to-call-her? dilemma. He'd see her at work in the morning, thank her again for her favor, then it would be business as usual.

It was a good plan, a solid plan. He liked plans.

"When will we break up?" Sara Beth asked as they walked to his car.

"When you're fed up with my lack of attention." *As usual.* The most common complaint he heard from women as they exited his life was, "You forgot I existed."

He didn't mean to. It just happened. He put most of his energies into his research. He had a good reason to find a solution to male infertility issues soon. A very good reason.

Yes, he wanted to help mankind, but he particularly wanted to help one man. Until then, Ted had given up his goal to be more social for a personal vow instead, a promise to devote his time and energy to the cause, putting his personal life on hold until he'd accomplished his goal.

Even though he felt ready—more than ready—to

marry and have children, he would delay it. He couldn't give his time to anything else but his research, nor ask a woman to sacrifice time with him so that he could reach his personal goal.

As Ted navigated streets and bridges, he gave Sara Beth a summary of his life. "Only child. Raised by strict but kind parents. Too clumsy to play basketball, even though everyone expected me to because of my height. Total nerd. Or geek. Take your pick of insult. I participated in all the science fairs and academic decathlons."

"And did very well, I'm sure," Sara Beth said.

He shrugged. Bragging wasn't part of his makeup.

"I wanted to get away from home after high school graduation, so I went to Stanford. I met Chance there. We were opposites in most ways, but both of us were determined to make a difference. We teamed up at the Breyer Medical Center in San Francisco and made some progress, but we didn't have the freedom to work in the way we needed. When Paul Armstrong extended the offer to come here, we said yes." Immediately. No hesitation at all. "How about you?"

"I'm also an only child, and my mother was strict but kind, but I was a jock. Played soccer from age five through high school and loved it. I didn't have any interest in leaving home, which is why I went to BC, and because of the institute's scholarship. I'd been working there since I was sixteen, starting as a part-time file clerk. I've never worked anywhere else."

"So you work there because you feel obligated?"

She didn't say anything for a while, then, "In some

respects that's true, but I believe in what they do, and it's a comfortable place for me. Lisa and I have been best friends all our lives, and so I spent a lot of time at the Armstrong home. I know her sister and brothers. Her father was always very kind to me, and my mother loved working for him. In fact, she was his first employee, was even kind of a girl Friday as well as his nurse until they got so big they needed more help."

She sat up straighter and looked around as he turned onto his parents' street. "Um, where are we?"

"Mount Vernon Square."

"As in, Beacon Hill?" she asked, sounding slightly short of horrified.

"Yes."

"I see," she said tightly. "And where do you live?"

"Back Bay."

She closed her eyes for a moment, then glanced at her dress. "Are you sure I'm dressed up enough?"

"You look fine." He almost said *beautiful,* which was the truth, but caught himself in time figuring she wouldn't believe him.

She went silent. He continued to talk as if nothing had changed, offering more family information, asking more questions of her, getting subdued answers. But when they arrived, he felt prepared to answer the basic questions his parents might put forward.

Ted let himself and Sara Beth into the 150-year-old Victorian house where he'd grown up. Inside, he pressed a hand to the small of her back and urged her toward the sitting room, where he could hear voices. He was appreciating the curve of her spine when he felt her stiffen a little. "They don't eat guests for dinner," he said close to her ear.

She laughed quietly, shakily.

"They've found that guests make for a better dessert," he added just as they walked through the open door.

Conversation stopped. His gaze swept the room. His mother and father were side by side on a settee.

But they were not alone.

Chapter Three

Sara Beth wanted to jab Ted in the ribs. Hard. Obviously he hadn't warned his parents he was bringing her, because they quickly glanced at a woman about Ted's age seated in a high-back chair, wearing a Valentine-red, body-hugging dress. She was blond, curvy and regal-looking, the silver spoon in her mouth invisible but obvious in her demeanor.

"Darling," his mother said as his father stood and came toward Ted and Sara Beth. "You brought a guest. How lovely."

Sara Beth gave her credit. She sounded genuinely pleased.

Ted shook hands with his father. "I thought I'd surprise you. This is Sara Beth O'Connell. Sara Beth, these are my parents, Brant and Penny Bonner, and a family friend, Tricia Trahearn."

Sara Beth caught a cool, speculative look from Tricia as they shook hands.

"It's been a long time, Tricia. How are you?" Ted asked, clasping her hand for a moment too long, in Sara Beth's opinion. Or was *she* doing the holding?

"I'm well, thank you. You're looking wonderful."

"I can't complain." He let go, then bent to kiss his mother's cheek. "Happy anniversary."

Shock surged through Sara Beth, then annoyance. Oh, yeah, she was going to get him for this. It was bad enough she seemed like a party crasher, but he also hadn't bothered to tell her it was his parents' anniversary.

"Thank you, darling," Penny Bonner said, lifting her glass to her husband. "Thirty-four years. Time does fly."

The only available seating was a second settee, facing his parents. Ted led Sara Beth there. She thought she was doing an admirable job of keeping her expression neutral, while an internal volcano threatened to spew. She'd accepted his invitation because she'd wanted an adventure, to recapture that piece of herself. Instead she felt like an intruder.

Which was Dr. Ted Bonner's fault, big-time.

Hadn't her mother warned her forever about doctors, particularly about doctors, love and romance? Yes, yes, yes. Forever. From as far back as Sara Beth's memory reached. Doctors lived in a world of their own, her mother had said. It was one of the reasons Sara Beth had kept away from Ted, since she'd been dazzled by an instant attraction to him. Nothing serious could ever happen between them.

"Glenfiddich on the rocks for you, I imagine, son?" his father said, then looked at Sara Beth. "What would you like?"

To dump a whole bottle of that pricey whiskey over your son's head. "White wine would be wonderful, thank you."

Brant moved to a bar cart, then returned with their drinks. No one spoke. The awkwardness grew by the second. Sara Beth didn't hazard a glance toward the sexy Tricia Trahearn, but felt the woman's interest. Or maybe she'd zeroed in on Ted. Either way, she didn't look anywhere but in their direction.

Sara Beth also wondered how irritated his mother was. Not only would she have to add another place at the table, there would be an odd number instead of even.

Ted's mother ended the silence. "Tricia is visiting her parents for a month," Penny said.

Penny was short for Penelope, Sara Beth recalled from Ted's conversation in the car. His parents were old Boston. *Very* old Boston, as in James-Bonner-arrived-in-America-on-the-ship-*Truelove*-in-1623 old Boston. Penelope and Brantley were family names from a long and duly documented genealogy through the centuries. Ted was officially Theodore, so named after ancestors from the eighteenth and nineteenth centuries. "It could've been worse," he'd told her as he'd parked the car. "Several were named Percival."

"How are your parents?" Ted asked Tricia, swirling his drink then taking a sip.

"Disappointed in me, as always."

"Why's that?"

She recrossed her legs and bounced her foot. "I haven't married and procreated yet." She offered a small toast. "I'm sure you've heard the refrain."

Sara Beth didn't appreciate Tricia's lack of subtlety, nor the way she seemed so familiar with Ted.

Ted smiled, returning the gesture with his glass. "Tricia is a judge," he said to Sara Beth. "Youngest on the bench at the moment."

Of course she is. Probably everyone he knew held positions of power and influence. Sara Beth was proud of where she came from and what she'd accomplished, but this was a whole new world to her.

"*Appointed* judge. Not here, but in Vermont," Tricia said. "We'll see what happens come election time."

"It'll be a landslide," Penny said with assurance. "And for the record, we don't pester Ted about marrying and procreating, as you so bluntly put it, do we, darling?"

"I suppose one would have to define the word *pester,* Mother," Ted responded, but with a smile. His father laughed.

"So, where did you and Sara Beth meet?" Penny asked.

"She's the head nurse at the Armstrong Fertility Institute."

"You work together?"

"Not together, exactly. I'm research. She's medicine," Ted said.

Sara Beth was fine with the fact he was fudging the truth a little. They weren't a couple, after all, and they wouldn't officially be working together until tomorrow morning.

"Do you help deliver babies?" Tricia asked.

"We don't do deliveries at the institute. We use the hospital next door. A lot of specialized staff and equipment is necessary, since we often have multiple births. I do, however, attend some of the births. Some of our patients find it comforting to have a familiar face present," Sara Beth explained.

"You enjoy your work?" Penny asked.

"I— Yes, I do. I've known since I was a child that it was what I wanted. I'm sure the decision was influenced by my mother, who was head nurse at the institute since Dr. Armstrong started it. She retired recently."

"And your father?" Penny asked.

Sara Beth wondered if Ted knew her background. In the car she'd only mentioned her mother, and he hadn't questioned her about her father. "My father has never been part of my life." *But maybe he will be. Maybe I'll find him, after all. The vault could hold the answers....*

She realized how quiet the room had gotten. No one knew what to say. "My mother and I are very close, though. How did you two meet?" she asked, diverting the conversation to his parents.

Brant laid his hand over Penny's. Love and affection radiated from her face, and it made Sara Beth hunger for someone to look at her that way. She'd been in a position to observe a lot of couples through the years, couples who were usually under a lot of stress, either trying to get pregnant or waiting out a complicated pregnancy, so they didn't always glow. Still, it was wonderful to see a husband and wife so obviously in love after so many years.

"Our mothers were in Junior League together," Penny said. "Brant and I hated each other on sight."

"We were four years old," Brant said. "She was annoying."

"And he annoyed."

"When did it change?" Sara Beth asked.

"On my sixteenth birthday," Penny said. "His parents made him come to my party."

"I did my duty and asked her to dance, a fast dance where we wouldn't touch, but the song ended right away and a slow one started. I felt stuck."

"That was all it took," Penny said, her smile warm as their gazes met. "The moment we touched—"

"Pow." He stroked her hair. "I stole a kiss later, and that was it for me."

"Same here."

Sara Beth glanced at Ted. He was looking into the distance, probably devising some chemical formula in his head—or maybe planning when he would see Tricia again. Or maybe he'd just heard the story too many times for it to have impact. To Sara Beth it was incredibly romantic.

By the time the party moved into the dining room, another place setting had been added. They were served an incredible meal by a small, wiry, white-haired man named Louis, who looked to be in his eighties and who winked at Sara Beth when she'd momentarily been overwhelmed by the situation. She relaxed then and enjoyed the seared salmon with ginger-lime sauce, roasted asparagus and brown rice with scallions. Dessert was carrot cake, an anniversary tradition because it had been Brant and Penny's groom's cake.

Conversation happened around her. Questions asked and answered, memories shared. "Remember when?" became Tricia's catchphrase, grating in Sara Beth's ears after the third time. And since Sara Beth didn't know enough about Ted, nor did she have a history with him, she couldn't counter anything Tricia said with a memory of her own. Ted didn't seem to notice, just nodded and kept eating.

"Remember the time we sailed to Providence?" Tricia asked Ted as Louis cleared the dessert plates. "We capsized," she said to Sara Beth. "He saved my life. My hero."

"You know, I've think we've bored Sara Beth with history for long enough," Ted said. He set his hand on the back of Sara Beth's chair, gave her what seemed like a tender look, almost bringing tears to her eyes, even though she knew he was only putting on a show for his parents.

She stopped being mad at him.

"We should be going," he said.

"Me, too," Tricia said, patting her lips with her napkin.

Their farewells were brief. "I'm sorry you didn't know ahead of time that I was coming," Sara Beth said to Ted's parents.

"Please don't concern yourself," Penny said. "We were thrilled he brought you. Truly, Sara Beth, your presence was a lovely gift."

Ted and Sara Beth left the house with Tricia, after Ted helped the woman into her coat. Sara Beth had figured out they must have dated in high school, and had seen each other at some point since, but none of Tricia's remember-whens seemed recent.

"Maybe if we both get after him," Tricia said, looking over her shoulder at Sara Beth, "Ted will finally furnish his loft. Penny says it reminds her of a college student. Do you agree?"

Sara Beth debated whether to admit she hadn't seen his place. "He works a lot." She felt Ted's hand cup her shoulder and squeeze.

"I heard. Penny wanted me to volunteer to take on the job of decorating for him. I have a knack for that sort of thing."

"I'll get around to it," Ted said.

"You've apparently been saying that for months."

"And I've meant it for months. When things lighten up at work, I'll take care of it."

"I already promised to help him," Sara Beth said, fed up with how the woman kept pushing.

To his credit, Ted didn't blink an eye at the lie. He just lowered his arm to Sara Beth's waist. His hand felt hot through her coat, which was an impossibility, she knew. Still...

"Really?" Tricia's brows arched. She looked Sara Beth over again, as if examining her for some kind of decorator gene—and coming up empty. "Why didn't you just say so, Ted?"

"He's a man," Sara Beth explained. "He doesn't like to admit he can't do something, you know?" She felt him laugh beside her and felt warm despite the cold night.

"Well, here we are," Tricia said, stopping next to a silver BMW. "Maybe we could have lunch?" she asked Ted. "Catch up. For old time's sake. Just friends, you realize," she said to Sara Beth.

For old time's sake? Right. For *now*. Her interest in Ted was as obvious as the cut of her neckline—low and open for invitation.

"I don't have much free time," Ted said, squeezing Sara Beth's waist a little tighter.

She leaned into him and smiled at Tricia.

"I'm sure we can work something out," Tricia said. "Mother and Father would love to see you, too."

"We'll see."

"Ted and I met when we were children, too," she said to Sara Beth. "Just like his parents."

"Without the same results," Sara Beth said, fed up.

"Good night, Tricia," Ted said in a tone meant to shut down the conversation.

He maneuvered Sara Beth past her and headed for his car, his arm still around her waist, even though he no longer needed to put on a show. He'd touched her earlier, twice. First, he'd accidentally touched her breast, catching her off guard—and himself, she could tell. Then later, at his parents' house, he'd rested his hand lightly against her lower back. It had startled her, because it was deliberate. But looking back now, maybe that wasn't all. Maybe it was the touch itself, which had revved her up.

"Thanks for the save," Ted said as they drove off a minute later. "And for realizing I needed saving."

"You *were* looking a little desperate." She smiled. "I'm kidding. What is your home like?"

"It's the top floor of a converted warehouse with a rooftop garden. That I never use."

She sighed. "If I had a garden, I'd rarely be indoors."

"There's no garden in the backyard of your house?"

"There is, but I'm just the renter. It's owned by a horticulture researcher at Harvard. I'm not allowed to touch his garden. Everything's an experiment."

"How long have you lived there?"

"Three years."

"I was envying your sofa earlier. Reminded me I should order one myself."

"So your loft does looks like a college student's?"

"It's…minimalist."

She smiled at that.

"I don't even know what's kept me from getting it decorated. I could order furniture online, so it's not like I'd have to spend time going from store to store. I just haven't done it. Chance gets after me, too."

She hesitated a long time before she said, "I take it you don't entertain much." How personal was she allowed to get?

"I never entertain. I should be reciprocating invitations. My mother drilled that particular etiquette into my head. Until I furnish the place, I can't."

"What's your style?"

"It would still be minimalist, but also comfortable. I have art—paintings and other pieces that I've collected or been given. They're piled in a corner. I suppose it makes sense to decorate around them." He pulled up in front of her house. "Do you see parking anywhere?"

"You don't need to bother." She gathered her coat around her and opened the door. "I'll be fine."

He looked at her directly. "You've met my mother."

She laughed. "Well, she's not here to see your breach of etiquette. Really, Ted, you could end up driving around for fifteen minutes. I don't need to be walked to the door." This wasn't a real date, anyway, she reminded herself.

"Thank you for going with me tonight. You saved my hide." He reached over and pressed her shoulder, his fingertips grazing her neck.

Her breath caught. The air around her crackled. Neither of them moved. She wanted to kiss him, saw his gaze drop to her mouth and linger, his fingers twitching at the same time, then digging in a little. *Move,* she ordered herself. *Get out. Don't look back.*

She didn't budge. "So. I'll see you bright and early tomorrow," she said.

He pulled away his hand slowly, cold replacing the heat fast—too fast. She shivered.

"Until tomorrow, then," he said, smiling.

She climbed out of the car, leaning back in for just a moment. "Good night."

"I'll wait until you're inside."

She nodded, was aware of his gaze on her as she crossed between two parked cars, walked up the sidewalk, then climbed the front stairs. Should she turn around and wave? Of course. He was being a gentleman. She waved, although she couldn't see if he waved back.

When she got inside she leaned against the door, her legs wobbly. What had just happened? Was she caught up in Penny and Brant's story of love at first touch? She wanted the same fairy tale. The same happy ending. She'd wanted that for a long time.

But with Ted? A man who turned her on just looking at him? A man she worked with? A *doctor?*

She climbed the stairs, went into her dark, quiet apartment, then didn't bother turning on the lights, moonlight casting just enough illumination. She slipped off her shoes, hung up her coat and sat on her sofa, curling her legs under her. Her body felt alive. Needy. Aroused.

How could she work with someone whose smallest touch left her breathless?

Her phone rang. She picked it up from the coffee table, her hello sounding shaky, even to herself.

"It's Ted."

She gripped the receiver with both hands. Her heart began to pound, loud and fast. "Oh, hi."

"Listen, I—"

What? You felt it, too? You want me, too?

"Sorry. A car just cut me off. Um, I left some papers on your kitchen counter. Would you bring them with you tomorrow?"

She closed her eyes, more disappointed than she should let herself be. "Of course."

"Thanks. See you."

"Bye."

She'd seen him around the building for months and been able to control it. So why this reaction today? And then there was the fact he hadn't seemed to notice her at all until today. Or had he studiously been avoiding her, as she had been avoiding him?

All she knew for sure was that she needed to be very, very careful from here on. First and foremost, she wanted to get into the vault.

And she couldn't—wouldn't—let her attraction to Ted get in her way.

Chapter Four

In the lab early the next morning, Ted made room for Chance Demetrios to study his computer screen. Ted had arrived well before dawn, needing to get started on his lightbulb moment of the previous evening.

"You came up with this last night?" Chance asked.

"Yeah. A purely random thought."

"How did we miss it before?"

"Because it's been a process. We had to go through the previous steps to get to this point."

"I think you're onto something, Ted." Chance stepped back. "This could be the breakthrough."

"Maybe."

They'd worked together for so many years that they didn't need to say a lot, could interpret each other's expressions. Chance grinned; Ted just nodded, their reactions as opposite as everything else about them. Although they were about the same height, and had similar dark eyes and hair, Chance was powerfully built and social, and the black sheep of his dominant and wealthy family, whereas Ted rarely made waves. Opposite in many ways, but similar where it counted.

Because what they had in common was a need to find a viable treatment for male infertility, although neither had told the other why. And both were stubborn and independent, which made them a good team, each other's checks and balances.

"Has Derek Armstrong weighed in on having Sara Beth working with us?" Chance asked.

"He hasn't stopped by today. Maybe he doesn't know yet." Ted figured Derek would have an opinion, since he'd had an opinion on everything else that Ted and Chance were doing as they tried to protect the institute's name.

"Did you spend the night here again?" Chance asked, booting up his own computer.

"No." But that reminded Ted that he needed to order a bed frame, his box spring and mattress being too low to the ground for comfort getting in and out of bed. "I went to my parents' house for dinner. It was their anniversary. How about you? You sounded hopeful about your date on the phone yesterday."

"Here's a piece of advice, my friend. Never have a first date on Valentine's Day."

With a few keystrokes, Ted forwarded the new hypothesis to Chance's computer. "Okay. Why not?"

"Expectations are too high." Chance tapped a couple keys, then his screen matched Ted's.

"For what? Roses? Candy? Sex?"

"All three."

"Your expectations or hers?"

Chance laughed. "In this case, hers."

"And you turned her down?" Ted had observed Chance in action for years. He flirted in the same unconscious way that most people breathed. "Got a fever or something?"

"Or something."

Ted studied Chance, but didn't continue the conversation. They worked side by side, their shorthand of familiarity being enough to convey their thoughts. Suddenly, Ted smelled sweet lemons and discovered Sara Beth standing beside him, wearing tie-dyed scrubs in blues and greens.

Technically she'd been his Valentine's Day date, but without roses, candy or sex. Without any expectations at all. She'd been a good sport about it, too.

"Good morning, Doctors," she said, unobtrusively setting down an envelope with what he assumed were his papers from the night before.

He hadn't needed them—he had a near photographic memory—but he'd gotten worried when her lights hadn't come on in her apartment after he'd dropped her off. The only reasonable way he could make sure everything was okay was to call her, using the excuse of bringing his notes to work.

"Good morning, Sara Beth," Chance said. "Thanks for agreeing to work with us."

"It's my pleasure. I know how anxious you are to have the situation cleared up."

Ted didn't take his eyes off his monitor, but he said good morning.

"Your first appointment just arrived, Dr. Demetrios," Sara Beth said.

He saved his work and shut down the computer. "Did you have a nice Valentine's Day?"

Ted heard her hesitation and wondered if Chance did.

"Yes, I did, thank you. And you?"

"She didn't have a sense of humor."

"Ah. Too bad. That's a requirement of yours, I'm sure."

Ted looked at her in time to see her eyes sparkling.

Chance nodded solemnly. "Number one priority. That, and being a redhead."

"Uh-huh."

He raised a hand. "Honest."

She tapped her watch.

"I'm going, I'm going." He headed to the door. "See you later."

The obvious ease of their relationship irritated Ted. "I'll be right back," he said to Sara Beth then followed Chance out the door, stopping him.

"Sara Beth is going to be working with us every day. You need to treat her more professionally."

Chance's brows lifted. "I've worked closely with her for months, Ted. We joke around. You've heard of the concept, right?"

"Joking is fine. But not flirting." He was making an

ass of himself, and he knew it, yet couldn't stop it. "You got yourself in trouble for that before, remember?"

A deep frown settled on Chance's face. He leaned closer to Ted, keeping his voice low. "How could I forget? But I wasn't guilty then, and I'm not guilty now. So lay off." He walked away.

It wasn't the first argument they'd had, and undoubtedly wouldn't be the last, but their disagreements were usually about intellectual or scientific issues, which eventually were proved or disproved. Plus, they enjoyed challenging each other.

This was different. They never intruded on each other's personal lives. Never had any reason to.

Ted shoved his hands through his hair, taking a few seconds to vanquish the irrational thoughts, then determine the reason for them.

Simple. He was jealous of how easy it was for Chance to flirt and tease.

Ted could learn, though. Tricia's presence last night had reminded him how far he'd come. In high school they'd both been labeled nerds. She'd blossomed into a beautiful, poised woman to match the intelligence that had been there all along. And he looked a little more put together now, which got him dates without him trying much. Not that he held any woman's interest for very long—

"I'm on the clock here," Sara Beth said from the open doorway, apparently having waited as long as she could while he self-analyzed.

"Sorry." He returned to the lab, and went directly to

a corner desk. "I had boxes brought up from the vault." He pulled up a page on the computer screen. "All you need to do is enter the information from the files into this spreadsheet."

She stared at the image. He was distracted by her lemon scent again, realized it was her hair that smelled so good.

"This seems like a job that one of the data clerks could do," she said, hesitance in her voice.

"So it may seem, but it's much more than just entering data. Plus, we want to involve as few people as possible. You need to read the files, to understand the information that's there, not just statistics. We're looking for reasons why there have been so many more multiple births in the past few years than in previous ones. The institute's protocols are exact. We don't allow more than three implantations, yet we've had more twins and triplets born than makes scientific sense."

She looked up at him. He'd gotten so close, he could feel her body heat, but he didn't move away from it. Neither did she.

"And because we had a big turnover of personnel after Dr. Armstrong retired, the people involved are gone and you're left holding the bag?" she asked.

"Not exactly, since we haven't been here long enough to blame, but Chance and I came here because of the institute's great reputation and what seemed to be unlimited funding. A scandal, which this is brewing to be, could cause a huge loss of funding, which could mean the death of our research." He almost brushed back a wisp of Sara Beth's hair that had escaped her braid.

"Okay. What am I looking for?"

He pointed out the items she should review, flagging anything questionable. "If you come across something that doesn't make sense or falls outside the category parameters, just ask. I'll be working in the lab all day."

She nodded. "When I'm done with these, should I go into the vault for more? I mean, how far back are we checking?"

He finally stepped away slightly. "I don't know yet. We may end up entering everything, converting all of it into the new program, something that would've been done, except that Dr. Armstrong said it wasn't necessary. Lisa and Paul want to bring the institute into the twenty-first century."

"Sounds like a good idea."

Ted wondered about her mood. She'd gotten quiet and businesslike since Chance had left. "Thanks again for last night, Sara Beth. I think I'm off the hook with my parents for a while."

"It wasn't a hardship for me." She fidgeted. "You and Tricia go way back, I guess."

He adjusted his lab coat. "We dated in high school." He remembered their first kiss, glasses bumping glasses. He hadn't known where to put his hands, so he hadn't made any attempt. They'd just sort of leaned toward each other and touched lips. They'd gotten a little better at it through trial and error, but it wasn't until he'd dated an older woman as a sophomore in college that he'd learned what he'd been missing.

"You haven't seen each other all these years?"

"Once, right before I graduated from Stanford." They'd slept together. She'd come to town for the sole purpose of sleeping with him, she told him, as forthright as always. It had been physically satisfying but left him feeling hollow at the same time, as if they'd needed to do it in order to move on with their lives, to prove to each other how far they'd come. That she'd shown interest in him last night was both surprising and uncomfortable. "She could be elected president someday. Or at the very least, be a Supreme Court justice."

"You can say you knew her when. Reporters will track you down to interview. You'll have your high school yearbook photos splashed on the tabloids and across the Web."

"My fondest wish," he said dryly.

She laughed, a bubbly sound that infiltrated his body and danced inside him, making him feel…edgy. He remembered the firmness of her breast against his hand, the tempting curve of her lower back…

Tempting? There was no denying it. She tempted him, even with her hair in a tidy braid, her bright scrubs and practical shoes.

"Would you go shopping with me?" he asked.

"Pardon me?"

He liked the way her eyes widened when she was surprised, her lashes long and dark. "I thought I'd look at furniture this weekend. Would you turn your lie into a truth by helping me?"

A long pause ensued, then finally, "Do you think that's a good idea?"

"I wouldn't have asked you otherwise. Why? Do you think it isn't?" He hadn't thought it through. The idea had struck, and he'd asked.

"We work together."

Ted was unprepared for the blow of a rejection. He rarely asked anyone for help doing anything, but he also couldn't remember being turned down before, either. "If you don't want to, just say so. It's not like it's a date."

Her gaze drilled his. "I'm sure Tricia would be glad to have you change your mind and ask her. She seemed ready and able."

"If I'd wanted to ask her, I would have. It could be fun, Sara Beth. An adventure," he added, appealing to that side of her.

They stood staring at each other. He waited her out.

"Okay," she said. "I need to see your loft first or I won't be able to picture the furniture in your space. I'm not a pro, you understand."

"You have good taste. Actually, anyone probably has better taste than me, but your apartment is comfortable. I want comfortable."

"And a place you can invite people over."

"Yes."

"Even if you don't really want to," she added, her eyes dancing with laughter.

They barely knew each other, but she'd figured him out. And he'd asked her to help him with the furniture because he'd already relaxed with her. She was easy....

No. That was a complete lie.

She was trouble.

Chapter Five

Sara Beth let herself into her mother's house at six o'clock on Tuesday night. No scent of food greeted her, which meant they would be eating out. "I'm here!" she called, then shut the front door.

"Be out in a sec," came Grace O'Connell's reply from her bedroom at the back of the house.

In reverse of Sara Beth's housing situation, Grace owned her two-story Victorian, lived downstairs and rented out the second story to a Harvard law professor. It was the house where Sara Beth grew up.

"Cute blouse," Grace said. "You actually shopped."

"Guilty." Sara Beth hugged her mom, wondering as usual if Grace was ever going to age. Although sixty-two, she looked much younger, her hair long, straight and blond, her few wrinkles mostly laugh lines fanning from the corners of her crystal-blue eyes. She and Sara Beth could trade clothes, if they wanted, they were built so similarly.

Sara Beth adored her. She'd had a wonderful childhood, had never felt denied anything—except a father, or even a father figure. If her mother had dated, Sara Beth never knew about it.

"How come you didn't call me to shop with you?" Grace asked, stepping back to look at her daughter more closely. "I would've been happy to go along."

"I didn't plan it. I found myself in front of the Gap yesterday. Everything was on sale. I still spent way too much."

Grace cocked her head. "Who is he?"

It wouldn't do any good to hold back. Her mother could spot a lie every time. "It's not what you think."

"Anytime a woman who hates to shop goes shopping, and buys more than she thinks she needs, there's a man involved."

"You buy new clothes all the time. I've never seen evidence of a man."

"I *like* to shop." She slipped into her coat and stuffed her wallet into a pocket. "Did you buy new lingerie?"

Sara Beth almost choked. "No, Mother. I did not."

"You're blushing. Hmm. That's interesting. Tell me about him."

"We're just friends."

Grace rolled her eyes, hooked her arm in Sara Beth's and headed toward the door. "Which is the most pathetic lie in the lexicon of dating."

"It's the truth in this case. I did go to a family dinner with him last weekend, but he called it a rescue date. His parents get on him about still being single and I went as a decoy." And ended up being aroused by his touch. Not exactly within the definition of "friend."

Outside, Grace slid her key into the lock. "So, he used you? How charming."

"I said yes because it suited my purposes, Mom, not his. I've gotten in a bad habit of staying home, especially now that Lisa practically lives at the institute. I decided to shake up my routine." She smiled. "So, where are we going?"

"Don't change the subject, young lady."

"There's no subject to change. Nothing's going on." They turned right at the end of the walkway. Sara Beth guessed they were going to Santini's, a small family-style restaurant two blocks away.

"Are you going out with him again?"

Sara Beth managed not to sigh. "Not on a date. I'm going to help him shop for furniture for his place on Saturday."

"Why?"

"Because he asked." *And because I want to.*

"Why aren't you telling me who he is, Sara Beth? If it's no big deal—"

"It's Dr. Bonner, okay? Ted Bonner."

Grace's brows arched. "The new research doctor?"

"Yes. I'm on a special assignment to help him and Dr. Demetrios, at Lisa's request."

"Somehow I doubt that includes tending to their personal needs."

"Look, Mom. It's a change of pace, something new to do."

"And you bought new clothes."

Sara Beth threw up her hands. "Because you'd been after me for months to do so. Now that I have, you're making a federal case out of it."

"Not about the clothes, sweetheart, and you know it."

"I remember all your lessons, Mom. All of them. Don't date doctors and especially don't fall in love with them. I got it. I've heeded it. Is that a new hairstyle?" she asked lightly.

Her mother laughed. "All right. I'll lay off. For now."

"Forev—"

"It's a little shorter," Grace said, fluffing her hair. "And just a tad blonder."

While her mother relayed the latest gossip from her hairstylist, Sara Beth debated whether to bring up the subject of her father…donor. She really didn't want to resort to sneaking a look at her mother's file, breaking rules, risking the chance of getting caught, but she'd waited long enough. And the opportunity to learn about her father might never come her way again.

But just then they arrived at Santini's, and the moment passed, at least for now. It wasn't a subject she could bring up in a public venue, especially if her mother got as angry as she had the other times Sara Beth had asked.

So they settled into noncontroversial topics for the rest of the evening, then on the walk home, Grace said casually, "I won't be able to have dinner next Tuesday."

"How come?"

"I'm going to Cancún for a week. I leave on Saturday."

Is she blushing? Sara Beth wondered, eyeing her. "Who're you going with?"

"No one. I just wanted a break from winter."

"You're going *alone?*" She and her mother had traveled together a lot through the years, but mostly driving trips to the shore.

"Would you like to come?"

"I can't. Not right now. But why didn't you ask earlier?"

"I decided this morning. I found an incredible deal for an all-inclusive resort. I've never done anything like this, and I'm excited about it."

Something wasn't ringing true, Sara Beth decided. On the surface, maybe her mother was being honest, but there was more to it.

"E-mail me your itinerary," Sara Beth said, giving her mother a hug. Maybe after the trip, she would open up. "And have fun. Remember your sunscreen. I do envy you a week of sunshine."

"And margaritas."

"That, too."

During the bus ride home, Sara Beth tried to examine her mother's announcement. She wasn't a spur-of-the-moment person. Like Sara Beth, her mother analyzed, planned, then finally executed, usually to unsurprising results. Taking off for Cancún on only a few days' notice was shocking enough, but to go alone?

Sara Beth's cell phone rang as she stepped off the bus at her stop.

"Hi, it's Ted. I hope I'm not disturbing you."

She knew his voice already, the deep, even tone that shot a thrill through her. The voice she hadn't dared to hope she would hear. "No. Actually you're keeping me company."

"In what way?"

"I just got off the bus and I'm walking home. What's up?"

"You know that stack of catalogs and magazines you gave me today?"

"Of course." She'd asked him to thumb through them and turn down the pages of what appealed to him, then she could figure out where they needed to shop.

"I'm not seeing anything I like."

"Nothing?" She'd given him everything from *Pottery Barn* and *Restoration Hardware* catalogs to *Architectural Digest* magazines.

"Does that mean it's hopeless?" he asked.

"I don't know what it means. Maybe I'll know more when I see the art you want to display." She was curious about his loft, too, was looking forward to seeing where he lived. "Or maybe what it means is you should take Tricia up on her offer to help. Or hire a real decorator."

He didn't respond immediately. "Let's see what we can do first. Where are you?"

"Not far from home. Why?"

"Can you see your house?"

"No, but I will in a few seconds. There. It's in view. Why?"

"Just trying to get a picture of how far you'd gotten." His tone was casual, but—

It hit her then. He was watching over her. He was keeping her on the phone until she was safely home. Maybe he gave his mother credit for drumming etiquette into him, but this wasn't etiquette. This was a character trait, one she valued, and probably deeply ingrained in him.

Sara Beth was raised to be independent, like her mother. They'd never had a man around to help. It was always just the two of them, or the handyman they hired occasionally when a job was beyond their skills.

"I'm turning up my walkway," she said, letting him know she knew what he was doing. "Climbing the first step. The second. Third. I've reached the landing."

She heard him laugh softly, so she put a little drama into her voice. "I'm inserting the key in my lock. Oh, look! It's turning. I'm opening the door. Now I'm shutting it—"

"And locking it."

She put her phone next to the bolt as it fell into place. Locked.

"Did you hear that?" she asked.

"You're making fun of me."

"No." And she wasn't. Warmth at his concern wove through her. She swallowed, not knowing what to tell him, so she just continued on with her running commentary. "I'm climbing the indoor stairs…unlocking my door…going inside…shutting and locking it. Done. Thank you. I couldn't have managed it without you."

He laughed.

"No, seriously, Ted, that was very thoughtful of you, walking me home."

"That's what friends are for."

Friends. She toed off her shoes and sank onto her sofa. "I was coming back from dinner with my mom. We generally get together on Tuesdays."

"That's…nice?"

She laughed at how he turned it into a question. "Unlike you, my mom doesn't pester me—that was the word, right? *Pester?* Anyway, she's not after me about getting married." But Sara Beth felt ready. She didn't want to wait—had no reason to wait, in fact. She had a good job and money in the bank, had dated enough to know what she was looking for and who not to waste her time on.

"Which is why you see your mother every week, and I don't do the same."

"For my mom and me, it's a routine," she said, considering it. "We started the Tuesday-night dinners when I moved out after graduation six years ago, so it's not just a routine but an ingrained habit now."

"Like me not having furniture. I'm almost used to it."

"We'll figure out something. Maybe you can show me what you don't like."

"I'd be dog-earing almost every page. Well, I just wanted to warn you that the job may be harder than you were planning on. Might take longer than you think. I mean, if you have a date on Saturday night, tell me what time you need to be home."

She hated admitting she didn't have a date. He already knew she hadn't had a date on Valentine's Day. "I don't have plans."

"I appreciate your help, Sara Beth. You've been a good sport. See you tomorrow."

She hung up the phone with a sigh. A good sport. He wasn't the first man to call her that. Men enjoyed her company, and usually wanted to stay friends so that they could continue to unburden their personal woes on good-sport Sara Beth, who was a good listener, non-judgmental and accommodating. And here she was, repeating the pattern.

Technically he's your boss. At least until this project was done. Which was an excellent reason for just being a good sport, she reminded herself, particularly since her body tingled around him.

She could always step back. If, after Saturday, she felt too drawn to him, too attracted, she could say no if he asked her to do anything outside of the institute.

But…would she?

The next morning Sara Beth felt her pulse rev and her face heat as she walked down the hall toward the lab. She bent over at a water fountain outside the room and took a long drink, stalling. The anticipation of seeing Ted had made falling asleep hard, then she'd found herself awake an hour before her alarm went off.

Straightening, she swallowed the cold water, then caught a glimpse of Ted through the window as she pressed the back of her hand to her mouth. He was wearing his glasses and lab coat, his hair tousled as if he'd plunged his hands into it more than once. From frustration? Impatience?

Then Derek Armstrong moved into view, coming up beside Ted to look at his computer screen. Sara Beth frowned. Why was he there? As CFO of the institute, Derek wouldn't normally drop in on the research doctors. There wouldn't seem to be a reason for him to do so.

Even though Sara Beth had spent a lot of time in the Armstrong home, Derek and his twin brother, Paul, were eight years older. She'd lost track of them until she'd come to work full-time at the institute. She did know that Derek and Paul were opposites in many ways, ways that made Paul a good chief of staff, respected and liked, and Derek more hard-nosed, since he was the money guy. But he hadn't endeared himself to the staff.

Or at least not lately. People hadn't whispered behind his back until recently. His expression was stern now as he talked with Ted.

Suddenly Ted looked toward the window. Sara Beth pulled back before he could see her watching. She didn't know why she was nervous about seeing him this morning, except that as she'd gotten to know him more each day, she'd found more to like each day, too. Her last boyfriend, a six-month relationship that had ended a couple months ago, would never have kept her on the phone until she was safely inside her house. He'd always "respected her independence," as he'd put it—perhaps because she'd made sure he knew her independence was something she prided herself on.

But after last night she'd altered her thinking a little. Being independent didn't mean she couldn't let a man be considerate.

Ted had made her feel special. With a simple gesture he made her previous boyfriends seem uncaring. And Ted wasn't even her boyfriend.

Derek came out of the lab, smiled slightly at her, then held the door for her to enter.

"Good morning," Ted said, his posture a little stiff.

"Hi," she said, going straight to her desk, upon which was the shopping bag full of catalogs and magazines she'd brought him the day before.

"I found a few possibilities online and printed them off," he said. "Some styles that appealed to me. They're on top."

"That's great." She pulled out the papers, glanced at them, then nodded. "It's you."

"I don't know what's me, exactly, but I liked it."

"Casual elegance, clean lines, masculine, not fussy. That's you." She set the bag on the floor. "I'll come up with a list of stores to check out."

"Thanks. I really appreciate it. Why don't I pick you up around nine on Saturday?"

She hadn't looked at him yet, but kept herself busy turning on the computer, taking off her jacket and hanging it up. She would finish up the first stack of files today. Would she get to go to the vault and grab new ones?

"It's an easy shot for me on the bus, Ted. There's no sense in driving to my house only to drive back to yours."

"I don't mind."

Out of the corner of her eye she saw him move toward her.

She finally looked at him. Big mistake. Even with his

nerd glasses and lab coat on, he looked sexy. Crazy sexy. Like she-wanted-to-kiss-him-for-hours sexy.

"Are you all right, Sara Beth?"

Desire and guilt battled for control in her head. She couldn't tell him how hot she found him, nor could she tell him that the moment she was allowed into the vault, she would do something completely unethical. For a woman who'd always prided herself on her integrity—

"Sara Beth?"

She sat. She didn't want to come across as rude, but she really needed him to go away. "I'm just anxious to get to work."

He didn't go away. In fact, he moved closer, into her personal space, stealing her oxygen. "Have you changed your mind? Would you prefer not to help me shop?"

She shook her head. Once she made a commitment to someone or something, she followed through. But this would be it, she decided. One time only. "I just don't think you need to pick me up on Saturday."

He stared at her. She stared back, trying to keep her expression bland.

"Good morning, all," Chance Demetrios said as he breezed through the door. He came to a quick stop and looked from Sara Beth to Ted. "Everything okay?"

"Apparently," Ted said, then walked back to his computer.

Chance lifted his brows at Sara Beth. She smiled. "Something I can help you with?"

"I just sent Mrs. Jordan next door to be prepped for a C-section. I thought you'd like to assist."

She hopped up. "Absolutely. If you don't mind, Ted?"

"Someone special?" Ted guessed.

"Candy Jordan was my first patient when I started working here full-time. She went through seven implantations before it finally took, and now she's pregnant with triplets. I've held her hand a lot."

Ted gestured toward the door. "By all means, go."

She hesitated, then looked at Chance. "See you in a few." He left.

She waited for the door to shut. "I'll come back later and work," she said to Ted.

"You can skip a day. It's fine."

She couldn't get a handle on his mood. Which was probably fair, since she hadn't let him get a handle on hers. She moved up beside him. "I don't want to skip a day. I'll work later on."

"Whatever works out."

He hadn't stopped staring at his screen. She wondered if she'd offended him. "Does it bother you that I turned down your offer in order to ride the bus to your home?"

He made eye contact. "You're doing me a favor, Sara Beth. A big favor. The least you can do is let me pick you up."

So he *was* upset about that. "You're right. Thank you. Yes, I'd appreciate that." She said goodbye then left.

So. They'd had their first fight. She smiled. She'd

thought Ted was extraordinarily patient, but even his patience could be tested when he wasn't getting his own way.

Frankly, she was glad to see this new side of him.

And wanted to see a whole lot more.

Chapter Six

Ted considered patience his strongest asset, and his ability to concentrate a close second. He could spend hours doing one thing, and only one thing, not even taking time to eat. Patience intact, he got to Sara Beth's house a few minutes early, hoping that parking spaces would open up along the crowded street of homes on Saturday morning as people went off for the day.

He didn't have to wait at all, a car pulling out just as he got there. He parked but stayed in the car, knowing she would be watching for him, sure of that much about her.

He drummed his fingers on the steering wheel. She was surprisingly stubborn for someone known at the institute as a nurturer. He hadn't seen evidence of any nurturing toward himself....

Which was fine with him. He'd never liked women who hovered. Not only did Sara Beth not hover, she kept a good distance—except for that night at his parents' house, and technically, he'd closed that gap several times. Having her working in the lab had been fine, unless she came to him with a question, her lemony scent breaking his concentration even before she talked.

He wasn't used to having his concentration broken so easily. It should annoy him, he supposed, but instead he was comfortable. He'd felt comfortable with a number of women, but not ones he'd had interest in touching.

He wanted to touch Sara Beth.

The front door of her building opened. She came out wearing jeans and a beige jacket that came to midthigh. She was pulling on gloves. Her hair was down and tucked into her jacket. Her warm breath misted around her in the cold morning air. Something caught her attention overhead, and she stopped, shading her eyes, then smiled. A bird, probably.

He tried to remember the last time he had stopped to watch a bird.

All work and no play— Was he that dull?

He climbed out of his car, leaned on the top. "You're prompt."

"So are you."

"You say that as if it surprises you."

"I had a fleeting thought that you may get involved in something and forget me."

"Not a chance." *Not a chance in hell,* he thought, as she got into his car.

He climbed in, too, then held out a cup of coffee with cream, which he'd noticed was how she took it, and a chocolate doughnut with chocolate frosting. "Good morning," he said.

She yanked off her gloves, tucked them in her lap, then accepted his offering. She toasted him with the coffee cup. "It is now."

Her eyes sparkled above the rim. Something shifted inside him, not uncomfortably, exactly, although not completely identifiable.

Ted started the engine and pulled away, but caught her eyeing him. "What?"

"Do you even own a pair of jeans?"

"Of course I do. Why?"

"You're always so dressed up, that's all. This is Saturday. Play day."

"I play fine in these clothes." But it got him thinking. If clothes made the man, did that mean he never played? This would take some thought, he decided.

The trip to his loft didn't take long and was mostly silent as he spent the time wondering if she saw him as being uptight, while she enjoyed the coffee and doughnut during the drive. He ate when he was hungry, didn't much care what it was. It refueled him, which was the purpose of eating. But watching her savor the chocolate frosting by licking it off the doughnut—

He looked away and just drove. Hadn't he been the one to chastise Chance for his dalliances in the past? In the end, it didn't matter if you were innocent of making unwanted advances. If people perceived otherwise, you were dead in the water.

He pulled into his underground parking space, almost commenting about how quiet she'd been, then decided not to. She didn't seem bothered by their lack of conversation. Her smile was as bright as usual. There was no stiffness in her shoulders, if she was holding back anything.

"Nice to have permanent parking," she commented as he punched in the security code to his private elevator that would take them to the top floor of the converted warehouse. "My mom does, too. It's great having a car available at times. Makes it easy to take weekend getaways."

"Having lived in San Francisco for so long, easy access to parking was on my list of requirements."

"Along with what else?" Sara Beth asked.

"A view of the Charles. Although I don't know why, since I'm hardly here to enjoy it. Lots of open space. I don't like small rooms. They make me feel hemmed in."

"Are you claustrophobic?"

"I just don't like walls." The elevator stopped. The door opened to a large, although not massive space, with cherrywood floors, exposed ductwork, brick walls and floor-to-ceiling windows facing an amazing view of the Charles River.

"This is stunning," Sara Beth said, slipping off her shoes as he did, moving into the loft, shrugging off her jacket as she went. "I can see your dilemma about decorating it. You need to create rooms without using walls, so everything has to flow from one space to the next."

She eyed him. "Are you sure you don't want to use a professional? I don't know that I'm up to the challenge, given that my education in decorating comes from watching the Home and Garden channel."

"Let's give it a shot. If you still feel the same at the end of today, I'll do something else." The truth was, he wanted to spend the day with her. He hadn't spent a day with a woman since he'd moved back, and now he found himself relaxed, work not pounding his brain, a rare occurrence. He needed a little R & R, then could return to work refreshed.

"Okay," she said, wandering into the kitchen, a newly renovated contemporary space with dark wood-and-glass cabinets, glass-tile backsplashes, stainless-steel appliances and black, brown and gold granite countertops.

A folding camp chair sat in eerie loneliness by the front window, an upside down cardboard box placed next to it to use as an end table, along with one floor lamp. A flat-screen television was mounted above the fireplace.

"Spartan," she commented, flashing a quick grin.

"That's a nice way of putting it." He gestured toward the rear of the unit. "Bedroom and bath are down this way."

The bathroom was large, the shower walk-in, the floor porcelain tile and the counters the same granite as in the kitchen. The bedroom space could be closed off by pulling large planks of polished wood attached to an overhead rail, spanning from wall to wall.

She glanced into his huge walk-in closet, where long-sleeved dress shirts lined one side, in blue, white and cream. Slacks in black, brown and charcoal took up the rack below the shirts. A few suits. A tuxedo. Quite a few shoes. A couple of polo shirts. And one pair of jeans, never worn, tags attached.

"*How* long have you lived here?" Sara Beth asked as they returned to the living room.

"Don't start." After a week of her being mostly businesslike, he was enjoying her playfulness now. "Or no more doughnuts."

She laughed, the sound echoing in his almost-empty space. "You get what you pay for."

She pulled out a notepad and measuring tape from her purse, and they went to work drawing a floor plan to scale. Then he spread out his artwork along the living room wall.

"Eclectic," she said, tapping her pencil against her lips as she viewed the minigallery. "No wonder you can't settle on a style."

"If I have a gut reaction to a piece, I buy it, whether it costs fifty dollars or five thousand."

From her purse she pulled out a digital camera and took photos of each piece. He could see her mind whirling with possibilities. He wished he had that kind of spatial vision, to see what could be instead of what was. Chance frequently accused him of having tunnel vision. Ted had come to accept that about himself.

He also knew that same tunnel vision may very well be the reason he would someday find that rare treatment, something reliable, that had eluded researchers forever. A scientist had to be devoted and single-minded. He was both, and unapologetic about it.

Ted heard his name being called. Sara Beth stood in front of him, waving her hands and smiling.

"Where'd you go?" she asked.

"Sorry." His defenses went up. So many women had become frustrated with how often he ignored them while delving into his own thoughts.

"Saving the world?" she asked, her smile softening.

She didn't seem at all upset that he'd tuned her out. Maybe because they were friends, not dating?

"You don't do that when you drive, do you, Ted?"

"No tickets. No accidents."

"But how many did you cause?" She laughed as she scooped up her purse and dropped her camera in it. "I'll use your bathroom, then we can go, if you're ready."

"Sure."

She breezed past him, leaving her fresh scent in her wake. He watched her walk away, her stride purposeful, her shiny hair swinging between her shoulder blades. An image flashed of her naked, straddling him, and bending over, her hair brushing his chest, then his stomach…

His body clenched. He turned away and moved to the window. She hadn't had a date on Valentine's Day, nor tonight. So…maybe she wouldn't mind spending time with him, helping him take a break now and then from his cause. Someone to share dinner with, have a conversation.

Of course, in the meantime, he needed to do something about sex. Or the lack thereof, in this case. As in, not since he'd left San Francisco. He figured that was why he'd reacted so strongly to Sara Beth, the only woman he'd touched in months.

He studied a couple strolling along the river's edge, hand in hand. Tricia would be a safer bet, he thought. She was home for a month, dedicated to her career, wouldn't expect the long term from him. They had a history. No complications to speak of. Except…he felt proprietary about Sara Beth. Unreasonably so, probably, but true.

"Ready?"

He turned around. Sara Beth returned his look, a small smile stretching her lips, curiosity in her eyes. He wanted to back her up until her legs hit his bed and she tumbled onto it, and follow her down. He wondered what she tasted like. Did her bra and panties match the brightly colored scrubs she always wore, or was she a pristine-white or invisible-beige lingerie kind of woman? No hint of an answer came from her V-neck black sweater that plunged only far enough to have him wishing for more.

Sara Beth's smile faltered. "Are you upset about something?"

"No." He laid a hand on her shoulder, then let go immediately. "I apologize. I was deep in thought."

She cocked her head. "I wonder what it's like, living in your mind. It must be fascinating."

It was the wrong thing for her to say. No one had ever considered his tuning out to be anything but negative. To have her think otherwise made him want to get closer.

"You'd probably find a lot of twists and turns and dead ends," he said, encouraging her toward the elevator.

"Did anything come from the idea that struck you at my house last week?"

"Yes. Chance and I are working on it." In fact, he should be in the lab now, but was determined not to feel guilty about taking a day for himself. He wasn't sure how to find a balance between work and social life.

"What do you think of Derek Armstrong?" Ted asked when they were in the elevator.

"Because Lisa is my best friend, I've known him all my life, but we haven't spent time together in a very long time—he's so many years older than me. Why?"

They stepped out of the elevator and headed to the car a few feet away. "I'm just trying to get a handle on him. He drops in now and then, asks a few questions. But I report to Paul as chief of staff."

Ted unlocked the passenger door and opened it for her.

She paused before getting in. "Well, Derek and Paul are twins, but that's where the resemblance ends. I get the impression you don't trust Derek."

How much could he say? Derek seemed much more interested in how the research for the treatment was going than the investigation of what could cause the institute a lot of damage. It should've been the opposite at this point.

"I don't know him," Ted answered carefully.

"I watched you when Derek stopped by the other day. Your spine stiffened. You never took your eyes off him. And he didn't ask questions, he interrogated."

So, he hadn't been wrong about that. He wasn't just being defensive. Sara Beth saw it, too. "You didn't say anything."

"It wasn't my place."

"I value your opinions, Sara Beth."

"You and I have an unusual relationship," she said after he'd started the engine. "You're my boss for part of the day, my coworker most of the day and I guess we're also friends."

She'd summed it up perfectly. And she was right, it was unusual but also complicated. "You nailed it."

"Which means it's just as confusing to you?"

"I'm not losing sleep over it."

She laughed. "Okay, then." She pulled a small stack of papers from her seemingly bottomless purse. "I've got a list of furniture stores I think might be suitable."

"How long did you spend online doing that research?"

She shrugged. "I had fun. I hope your mother likes the results."

"It only matters what I think."

"I know, but…"

"No buts, Sara Beth. It's a fact."

"And facts matter most to you."

Yes, most of the time that was true. He liked facts. Good, solid, unchangeable facts made the world go around—his world, anyway.

But he was coming to like the mystery that was Sara Beth O'Connell, too, the woman he could already call a friend, but who also made him want.

Friends with benefits, perhaps?

Now, that was an idea worth getting lost in.

Chapter Seven

Sara Beth had occasionally wondered what it would be like to have a lot of money. Not that she felt she lacked anything, but how having a lot of money could affect someone's life.

Now she knew. Or to a degree, anyway.

Having money meant being allowed to buy floor models and have them delivered the same day instead of waiting weeks or months. It meant the owner waited on you personally. It also meant having a credit card with a large enough balance to charge just about anything, including a loft's worth of furniture.

Sara Beth had bought a piece at a time for her apartment over a couple of years, not wanting to get into debt, and often picking up secondhand pieces she would refinish or repurpose in labor-intensive, satisfying projects.

"Have you ever painted a room?" she asked Ted as they waited in the owner's office at Caro Miro's Design Studio, a high-end, contemporary furniture store—the sixth store they'd visited, and the most successful shopping they'd done. Caro was off arranging the delivery of a sofa, two side chairs, a dining room table and chairs, a sleek dresser to fit in his walk-in closet and a king-size bed frame and headboard. There was more to buy—tables, lamps, more chairs, a bedspread—but not today.

Ted stopped thumbing through a furniture catalog to look at Sara Beth, her out-of-the-blue question getting his full attention. "Painted a room? No. Why?"

"Just curious."

"Have *you?*"

"Lots. I don't like to paint walls or ceilings, but I don't mind doing the trim. You probably wouldn't even need a ladder." She sighed. Being tall had its advantages. "I'm thinking you should repaint the bedroom part of your loft a deep, warm brown. Are you up to it?"

"I believe in letting the experts do the jobs they've trained for."

She grinned. "I'll bet your father said that to you while you were growing up."

He cocked his head thoughtfully. "It does sound like him."

"So, you'll give it a shot?"

"Would you ask a painter to dissect a frog?"

She laughed. "When's the last time you dissected a frog?"

"In high school biology class." His eyes lit with humor. "If you think the walls should be painted, I'll have it done. As long as you choose the color."

"What do I get in return? I mean, I'm suffering for my generosity already."

"In what way?"

"My feet hurt. My back aches. And I'm hungry!" Before he got all serious or feeling guilty on her, she added, "But today was a whole lot of fun. I wouldn't have missed it for anything."

"We didn't always agree."

"Isn't that great?"

"You're strange." He softened the statement with a crooked smile.

She felt highly complimented. All her life, she'd been the least strange person ever. People could count on her to be unbiased, easygoing, and noncombative. If Ted saw her as something more lively—like strange—she was glad. She really was having an adventure. "Thank you."

He looked doubtful but said nothing because the owner/designer returned to the office.

"You're all set," Caro Miro said. She was a tall woman in her late thirties, wearing a vibrant blue outfit that hugged well-toned curves. Her catlike eyes zeroed in on Ted. "You'll have delivery by six o'clock."

"I appreciate it."

Sara Beth watched the interaction between the two. She'd come to realize that Ted had no idea how attractive he was. He never noticed when women stared, or flirted, which this one was doing, and he was missing all the signals.

"I thought I'd come with the delivery people to see your loft," Caro said, handing a credit card receipt to him to sign. "Then I would be able to make recommendations for the other pieces you're looking for."

Ted looked at Sara Beth then. "That won't be necessary. We seem to make a good team. But I do appreciate all the time you gave us today, and the quick delivery."

Sara Beth's heart did a little leap first, then she tried hard not to smirk at the much-sexier woman. Caro might be a few years older than Ted, but Sara Beth didn't think that would've stopped him from responding to her obvious flirtation if he'd been interested.

Which he wasn't—because he and Sara Beth made a good team. It wasn't her imagination or wishful thinking. He'd said so.

He started to sign, then stopped. "There's an error."

Caro used the opportunity to bend close to him. "Where?"

"You undercharged me by six dollars."

She pressed a hand to her chest and smiled. "Oh, for goodness' sake. It's not worth running it again. Consider it a thank-you."

Ted signed the slip, pulled out his wallet, drew out six dollars and handed it to her as he stood. "There."

Caro looked surprised. Sara Beth wasn't the least bit.

"Do you like Thai food?" he asked Sara Beth as they left the shop.

"Love it."

He pushed a speed-dial button on his cell phone and called in an order, requesting several dishes. She wondered how often he ordered in.

"At least I can take care of your hunger problem," he said, ending the call.

"Thanks." Darn. No back rub or foot massage.

When they reached the loft, Sara Beth pulled her "Ted" folder from her purse and set it on his breakfast bar as he headed to his bedroom to check his answering machine. She would've gladly flopped onto a sofa, if he'd had one.

"If you need to put your feet up," he called from the bedroom area, "feel free to use my bed."

Sara Beth froze in place, tempted. Too tempted. "I'm okay, thanks," she called back before she changed her mind. "Do you have any soda?"

"Maybe. Check out the refrigerator. Make yourself at home."

His refrigerator held several containers of take-out cartons and boxes, some orange juice, assorted condiments, three Cokes and two dozen eggs. "You've got Cokes. Do you want one?" she called.

"Sure," he said from right behind her.

She jumped. He'd come up while she'd been bent over staring at the contents. He set his hands on her waist and held her so that she wouldn't crash into him, but in doing so, her rear pressed against his pelvis.

She laughed as she stepped away, the sound shaky, then passed him a can.

"Let's sit down," he said. "The delivery people won't be here for a while." He guided her toward the canvas camp chair with built-in cup holders by the front window, made her sit there, then he sat on the floor, setting his can on the upturned cardboard box. He reached for her feet.

"What are you doing?" she asked, although pretty sure what his answer would be.

"Taking care of your second problem."

She was glad she'd decided to wear cute socks, the ones with the dancing polar bears, but she couldn't relax. What if he intended to massage her back, too? She would have to turn him down. She didn't want to, but she definitely had to.

Oh, but his hands felt good, his fingers strong, his thumbs finding the sore spots and releasing them with pressure. At work she was on her feet all day, but she always wore comfortable, cushioned shoes, instead of hard-soled ankle boots.

Sara Beth shut her eyes and swallowed the groans that threatened to escape her throat. *Pretend he's a doctor performing a treatment....*

Nope. That didn't work. He wasn't *her* doctor.

She opened her eyes a tiny bit, saw a peaceful expression on his face, as if he was enjoying himself, too. She wanted to run her hands through his long, wavy, soft-looking hair, then when he looked up at her, kiss him....

Dr. Ted Bonner fascinated her. When he set his mind to do something, he did it all the way, giving his complete attention. In bed, would he—

A buzzer rang, disrupting her escalating fantasy.

"Too soon for the food. Must be the furniture delivery. They're early," he said, hesitating for a moment, then standing and moving to look at a closed-circuit screen. He stepped into the elevator. "I'm sorry to cut the foot rub short."

Me, too. More than you'll ever know. She grabbed her soda, trying to look casual. Which worked until Caro came out of the elevator with Ted, talking animatedly, flirting outrageously. The woman didn't even have the sense to dial down the flirt volume when she saw Sara Beth.

"I was just explaining to Ted," she said, as he sent the elevator back down, "that he might not be happy with the rug you chose for the living area, so I brought a few more to look at, just in case."

"How thoughtful," Sara Beth said, keeping the sarcasm to a minimum.

"What a great space," Caro exclaimed. "You're going to need a lot more furniture, though, don't you think?"

"For now I'm going to live with what I got today," Ted said, "then decide what else I need."

Sara Beth was trying to get a handle on whether Caro was more interested in making sales or making Ted.

"I think that's a great idea." Caro moved to the window. "You have a fabulous view."

Ted winked at Sara Beth. She decided he'd figured out Caro just fine, was not as oblivious as he seemed.

When the elevator door opened, two burly men emerged then unloaded six large area rugs. The next hour was spent laying out each rug, rearranging the furniture each time. Their Thai food was delivered, Sara Beth's stomach growling as it sat on the counter, calling her name.

Finally they settled on the rug they'd originally chosen, the furniture was put in place, and his bed set up. Caro lingered, offering advice on what else he should consider. Ted committed to nothing, and finally got her out the door.

"I don't suppose you have place mats," Sara Beth said as she began heating up the food in the microwave.

He gave her a you've-got-to-be-kidding look.

"Paper towels?"

"I'll get them. You must be starving."

"I could eat the paper towels, I think."

He laughed. "She's quite a pitch woman, isn't she?"

Sara Beth shrugged.

"I know you have an opinion," he said.

"She's good at her job."

"Not really." He grabbed two plates and some silverware and set everything on the new dining room table.

"You bought a whole lot of stuff from her."

"I would've bought more if she hadn't been so pushy. Which means," he added, catching Sara Beth's gaze, "more shopping at different places to finish up."

So, he wasn't a pushover, wasn't just making choices to get the decorating over with. Good. "I'm available next Saturday."

"Thanks." He laid a hand over hers as she set a carton on the dining room table. "For today. For helping at the institute. For bringing a little fun into my life."

She swallowed. "Ditto."

"Ditto," he repeated, grinning, shaking his head. "Okay. You're welcome."

By the time they were done eating, hung a few pieces of art and made a list of everything else they thought he might need to buy, Sara Beth almost fell asleep standing up next to his bed, which they'd just made up. It was finally off the floor.

"So, you're not hungry anymore, I imagine," he said.

"Definitely not."

"And your feet feel okay?"

She wriggled her toes. "Fine."

"Which leaves your aching back."

Panic had her pulse thrumming in a hurry. "I'm rested. I feel good."

"You just spent a couple of hours climbing up and down ladders, and holding large pieces of art over your head." His smile was a slow burn, as if he knew how attracted she was—and how scared to give in to it.

Unless she was truly under the power of wishful thinking, he'd been testing the waters with her all day, making flattering comments, giving her the eye, smiling in that way that showed interest beyond coworker or friend, no matter what they labeled their relationship.

She waited for him to make it clear what he was after, but he didn't say or do anything. She decided to retreat, to think the situation over. "I should get home," she said, sidling around him to return to the living room.

"So soon?"

Sara Beth laughed. They'd spent twelve hours together. She stuffed her notebook in her purse. He swiped his keys from the counter, then stopped and looked around at the partially furnished living/dining room. "Already a big improvement," he said, eyeing the dark brown leather sofa and side chairs, the modern dining table and sleek nickel-and-leather chairs, and the red-and-brown area rug.

She nodded. "I have to admit I was feeling pretty cocky when you decided you liked the rug we picked out at the store best, instead of any of the others that Caro brought."

"When I make up my mind, I rarely change it."

"Even about decorating your place, apparently, which was way out of your comfort zone."

"I had great help." He tossed his keys lightly. "I may not have vision, but I know what I like."

"What do you suppose your parents will think?"

"It will only matter that it's done. And that my grandmother Holly's portrait of my mom as a little girl is up in a prominent place."

They took the elevator down and got in the car. "Want to stop someplace for dessert?" he asked, putting the car in gear.

"I couldn't eat another bite."

They drove in silence. She wished she knew if he was thinking about his new decor, her or his work. Most likely, work.

"Look at that," he said as they neared her house. "Parking right out front." He parallel parked, shut the engine off and opened his door.

By the time she got out, he was there, extending a hand, which she took reluctantly. "You don't have to walk me to my door. It's not like this was a date."

"Humor me." He let go of her hand.

They moved up the short walkway, climbed the stairs. She put her key in the door then turned to him. "I'll see you Monday morning."

He reached around her, turned the key and opened the door, then gestured for her to precede him up the second set of stairs to her apartment. She wouldn't invite him in. She absolutely would not, even though she had cookies and cocoa, the perfect ending to the day. She made herself stand in the open doorway.

"Good night, Ted."

She thought he was going to kiss her, but he wrapped his arms around her in an all-encompassing hug. She felt enveloped…and safe. His body felt familiar, when it shouldn't. She curved her arms up his back, pulling herself closer, feeling him from sturdy chest to hard thighs. He wrapped one arm around her midback, one a little lower, his fingertips resting on the upper curve of her rear. Her nipples hardened, wanting his touch, wishing he would pull her even closer. She barely resisted pressing her lips to his neck.

She was aware of everything about him—his strength, his heat, the promise of satisfaction for the building need inside her—but also that they worked together. That he was a doctor. That he came from old Boston money, had a place in a level of society she didn't know.

That a woman like Tricia Trahearn was much more suitable for him.

"Your friendship has come to mean a lot to me

already," he said, his breath disturbing her hair. He stepped back, his hands on her shoulders. "Thank you."

Friendship. The word righted her world again, put her in her place. She smiled brightly, probably too brightly. "You're welcome."

He went down the stairs and was gone, leaving her body aching and unsatisfied—and grateful. She was ready for marriage, a family.

She didn't need the complication of Dr. Ted Bonner.

Ted spotted Sara Beth standing in front window, watching him. He raised a hand toward her then got into his car without waiting for a return wave. He drove off in a burst of speed.

Why the hell had he hugged her like that? Let his hand drift down to the tempting curve of her rear? He'd been wanting to touch her since he'd come up to her bending in front of his refrigerator earlier, then later on when she'd helped him make his bed after the furniture men had left. She'd leaned over to smooth his sheets. He'd almost cupped that fine rear, had been stopped by her standing up, banging into him, a habit they'd gotten into, being clumsy around each other.

Friends with benefits. He'd been thinking about it all day, as she'd frequently gotten into his space, brushing against him to get a better look at something, smiling at him or pursing her lips as she studied a piece. She had a quick, easy laugh, light and joyful, and a slow, smoldering heat that appeared less often, but did appear, although he had to catch her off guard to see it.

And then there was the hug. He'd taken her into his arms without thinking, prepared to just give her a good-night hug, a thanks-for-everything short embrace. Then it had become something else. Even she had felt it. She'd moved closer to him instead of away. Her breath turned shaky. She'd gone up on tiptoe, which had aligned their hips. He'd pulled back before she could feel his reaction to her, had seen her nipples pressing against her T-shirt, an invitation he wished he could accept.

Friends with benefits. He needed to give that more thought. Sure, he wanted marriage—but not yet, not even anything close to it. If he took a break now and then from his work, it needed to be for fun, for pleasure, not with an eye toward the future, no matter how much he wanted otherwise.

For pleasure. The thought settled, a hazy fantasy that lingered as he parked and went up to his loft. He admired the newly decorated space for a minute, then decided to take a shower. His answering machine caught his eye, and he remembered the message from Tricia earlier, a call he'd ignored while Sara Beth was there.

Friends with benefits. Tricia would fit the bill, at least the benefits part, and without complications. She'd invited him to dinner next Sunday for his birthday. He had no doubt they'd end up in bed, if that was what he wanted.

And he wanted. But not Tricia.

He wanted Sara Beth O'Connell. Exclusively.

Chapter Eight

A few days later Sara Beth peered into Lisa's office. "You texted?"

Lisa gestured her in. "Shut the door, please."

She was looking more stressed each day, her mouth set, a furrow between her brows. It was hard for Sara Beth to see her this way.

"How about we go out tonight?" Sara Beth asked, sitting. "It's hump day. Half-price drinks at Shots. Free fries with the burgers." The always-crowded pub and grill was nestled in the center of the Cambridge medical community.

"I can't. I really wish I could." Wisps of Lisa's long hair had fallen around her face, a slight messiness that was rare for her, and it was only eight o'clock in the morning.

Sara Beth leaned toward her. "I miss you. And I'm worried about you. You've lost weight. You can't afford to lose weight."

"I'll be fine." She sat back, all business. "I need an update on your investigation, please."

Sara Beth frowned at the change of subject. "It's moving along. We've gone back five years so far. The statistics haven't been analyzed yet, and I think Ted wants to take it back further before we do. To uncover patterns, if there are any, before he comes to any conclusions. He wants a once-and-for-all conclusion. Don't you?"

"Of course. So, let's do this. I want you to free up more time, as much as you can manage. We need to get to the bottom of this *now.*" Her hands were clenched, her knuckles white.

Sara Beth studied her, the way she wouldn't make eye contact, the lack of a smile. "What's going on? There's more than just what Ted and I are trying to learn, which is bad, but not enough to stress you out to this degree."

"There are some money issues...." Lisa put her hands over her eyes and groaned. "Oh, God. I didn't mean to say that. Sara Beth, you can't say a word to anyone. No one."

"I won't. You know I won't." Fear whipped through her—about the institute, her job, her future. Everyone's future. They'd helped so many people to have babies. That couldn't end.

And then there was Ted, so close to making that dream a reality for even more people.

"Do you need me to tell Ted that I'm increasing your hours?" Lisa asked.

"I will. He'll be glad." She wished she could confide in her best friend, tell her about last Saturday and get her opinion. Tell her that Ted was on her mind all the time. All the time. Maybe the distraction would be good for Lisa, too. "Please come to Shots with me, Lisa. You need a break."

"Not tonight." Her phone rang, and Lisa picked it up, signaling the end of their conversation.

Sara Beth headed to the lab, urgency in her step, worried for Lisa, fearful for the institute…and anxious for the opportunity to get into the vault much sooner than she'd anticipated. Through the lab window she saw Ted and Chance in an intense discussion, not arguing, just extraordinarily serious. Chance didn't smile once.

She hesitated, then finally opened the door and stuck her head in. "Is this a bad time? Should I come back later?"

"That'd be good. Give us ten minutes, please," Chance said.

Ted turned and looked at her but didn't seem to register her.

She backed out, letting the door shut on its own, and leaned against the wall beside it. It seemed everyone was having some kind of crisis. And secrets.

Annoyed at being left out of the loop, she wandered away, deciding to get a cup of coffee from the break room. As soon as she'd poured a cup, she got a text message from her mother:

Hvng wndrful tme. Styng xtra wk. Love.

Which reminded Sara Beth that her mother had never sent an itinerary. She'd said that she wouldn't be out of cell-phone communication range, so what more did they need?

Which possibly meant her mother wasn't where she'd said she was going. Maybe she was with a man. More secrets.

She typed Have fun in the text box and sent it to her mother, not asking the questions she wanted to, not calling her, either, figuring it would go to voice mail.

Sara Beth sipped her coffee. Her life had gone from routine to unpredictable. She'd wanted to recapture some adventure, but the fun-and-games kind, not all this serious stuff.

After ten minutes, she returned to the lab, dumping her mostly full coffee cup, since food and drink weren't allowed. Ted and Chance were standing next to the centrifuge. Chance elbowed Ted, as if trying to get him to laugh, so Sara Beth felt free to go inside.

"Thanks for waiting," Chance said.

"No problem. Is everything okay?"

"Yes," Ted answered, still looking serious, but not grim—or somber, or whatever that was she'd seen on his face before. "Good morning, Sara Beth."

"Hi. I have good news." She didn't know what to do with her hands, so she slipped them into her pockets. "I've been cleared to give you a lot more time so that we can finish up as soon as possible."

"That's great," Ted said.

"I'm looking forward to getting back to normal

myself," Chance said. "Carrie's doing an admirable job of filling in for you, Sara Beth, but she's not you."

She smiled at the compliment. They did work well as a team. She respected him as a doctor. He was particularly good with the husbands, often counseling them separately through the in vitro process, knowing that most of the attention so often focused on the wives and their emotions. Sara Beth liked that he went the extra mile.

"So," she said, anticipation making her stomach do flip-flops. "I finished the latest box of files yesterday. Should I go to the vault and get more?"

"I already did," Ted said, pointing to the box next to her desk, which she hadn't paid attention to, thinking it was the old box. "I hadn't realized before, but I found out you're not authorized."

Not authorized? She could never go into the vault? Never find her mother's file? She grabbed her stomach, the pain so intense that nausea rose. She swallowed hard.

"Hey." Ted grabbed her as she swayed. "Sit down."

Chance rolled a chair behind her. She sank into it.

"What's wrong?" Ted asked, crouching in front of her, putting a hand on her forehead. "Are you sick?"

She waded through the agony in her mind to find an answer for him. "I…had cereal this morning. Maybe the milk was bad," she said, knowing it was lame, unable to think of anything else.

Chance had his fingers on her wrist. Ted was lifting her eyelids, checking each eye.

"Do you need to throw up?" he asked.

The absurdity of the situation struck her. Here she was being tended to by two doctors, all because she'd been denied access to information she had no legal right to have, anyway. How guilty would she have felt if she *had* gone into the vault and gotten that information? What would she have done with it? She couldn't contact the man after all these years, could she?

No, it was better this way.

And maybe at some point, she would actually believe that…

"I'm okay. Really." She gently pushed their hands away. "I don't know what happened, but I'm all right now and ready to get to work."

"Just sit there for a while," Ted said.

She would rather go somewhere and cry, get it out of her system, but she was sure they wouldn't let her out of their sight until they were satisfied she wasn't going to pass out. "Okay," she said.

The timer on the centrifuge went off. As Ted reluctantly left her, Chance whispered, "Are you pregnant?"

Shocked, she met his concerned gaze, her face heating up. "No!"

"Sure?"

"Yes. Positive."

He patted her shoulder, then joined Ted. Only a few words of their discussion reached her. *Experiment. Risk. Won't know until…*

Were they on the brink of success, then? Did they have something ready to try? Wouldn't there be all sorts of hoops to jump through for the government first?

She used her feet to push her chair to her desk and opened the box, pulling out a few folders, then turning on her computer, trying to accept defeat by reminding herself that when push came to shove, she may not even have followed through on her plan. She just wasn't sure she could live with doing something so unethical.

Sometime later Sara Beth felt herself in motion. Ted was pushing her chair to the lab door.

"What? Hey! What're you doing?" she asked, holding her feet up as they went.

"You're taking a break. You didn't hear me call your name five times. I think I've rubbed off on you."

Not yet, you haven't, but there's hope. The thought made her smile, as did his taking care of her, worrying about her.

"Go fuel yourself," he said as she stood. "I don't want to see you for at least a half hour."

"Breaks are fifteen minutes."

"Are you arguing with your boss?"

"No, sir. I just don't know how to take a half-hour break. I can do an hour for lunch, but a break? Can't."

He didn't roll his eyes, but he might as well have. "Whatever."

She laughed. "May I ask," she said, getting serious, "if you and Chance have discovered something new? Something exciting? I couldn't help but notice that you both seemed so intense."

"Maybe. That's all I can say at this point."

The look in his eyes gave a different answer. "You *did.*" She squeezed his hand. "I won't say anything, I promise." Yet another secret to keep. She grinned at his caution-filled expression then she left the room, knowing he hadn't shut the door yet and was watching her.

Her heart was lighter. Even though she'd hoped so much to see her mother's folder, she knew it would have weighed on her, too.

It was better this way.

Ted waited until Sara Beth was out of sight then he grabbed his cell phone and made the call he'd wanted to make for years.

"Hey, Ted. How's it going?" came the voice on the other end.

Caller ID had taken the element of surprise from phone calls, Ted thought. "Good. They're going really good."

A few beats passed. "Are you saying—"

"Nothing definite, you understand. But more hopeful than ever. Want to meet and talk about it?"

"You have to ask?"

Ted kept his gaze on the door, in case Sara Beth—or Derek—approached. Derek would be the last one Ted and Chance would tell.

"How risky is it, Ted?"

"If nothing else, it might actually make you healthier."

A quick, deep laugh came across the phone. "Not a chance. I've been preparing for this, following every detail of the regimen you put me on months ago. Vitamins, lots of sleep, eating well, exercise, no hot tub. I'm so healthy I should be the poster boy for it. Hell, Ted, I'm even doing yoga."

"Good. All those things help. But I don't want you to worry about risk. The compound is all natural— vitamins, minerals, protein enzymes, amino acids."

"Seems too easy."

"I know. Guess we'll find out in a few months."

"Okay. Man. Okay. Thanks, Ted. You don't know—"

"I do. Want to meet for dinner?"

"Yeah. How about six o'clock at Shots?"

Ted frowned. "Why there?"

"Noisy, anonymous."

"We could meet at my place. I even have some furniture now."

"Humor me."

Ted was confused but agreed. He wouldn't mind going out for dinner instead of having takeout. And he'd heard that Shots was the place to go. "You got it. See you then."

He hung up then dialed Chance. "Six o'clock at Shots."

"I'd prefer the Coach House. It's much quieter."

"His choice. He *wants* noise."

Ted slid his cell phone into his pocket. Now that they'd come this far, he wanted instant results.

So much for patience being his strongest asset.

"This is good," Lisa yelled into Sara Beth's ear. "Thanks for dragging me away."

"Purely selfish of me," Sara Beth replied, a partial truth, since she really believed Lisa needed a break, but so had Sara Beth after the day she had. Shots was the answer.

They'd shouldered their way into the fray of happy customers, found a small table and landed there. Sara

Beth had ordered a margarita in honor of her mother. Lisa was nursing a peach mojito. Burgers and fries would be up soon.

Sara Beth leaned back and surveyed the room. She always changed into street clothes before she went home, but plenty of people were wearing scrubs or at least the comfortable shoes they all tended to wear.

"We got a lot of work done today," Sara Beth said, leaning close to her friend. "I can see an end to the investigation."

"That's great. I hope that'll be it, and Chance and Ted can relax." She hesitated. "Well. Look who just walked in."

Sara Beth followed Lisa's gaze, spotted Ted and Chance with a man she didn't recognize. "Who's that with them?"

"I don't know. Attractive, though."

Sara Beth studied the man. He was about the same age as Ted and Chance, not quite as tall, but *attractive* wasn't a word she would use to describe him. Powerful and intense, yes. Alpha, yes. But, simply attractive? "They all seem really out of place. Doctors don't tend to hang out here." In particular, Ted didn't fit, Sara Beth thought, wondering if he would notice her and what would happen because of it.

But the crowd was dense, and they found their own table as a couple got up to leave. The only one facing Lisa and Sara Beth was Attractive Guy, and he was only looking at Ted and Chance, at least until the waitress went up to take their order. Then he looked around, his gaze landing on her and Lisa and holding for a few long seconds, long enough to make Sara Beth squirm.

"Intense conversation going on there," Lisa said as their burgers and fries arrived. They each took a big bite, nodded their heads at how good and juicy the burgers were, then Lisa picked up the conversation.

"So, what's new with you?" she asked.

"I'm falling for Ted." She hadn't meant to say it like that. She'd meant to dance around the topic, get some general advice. But she and Lisa were best friends. There wasn't much they didn't share.

"Ted? Him, Ted?"

Sara Beth nodded and bit into a hot, salty French fry.

Lisa sat back, looking stunned, then she smiled. "Wow."

"I know."

"Have you been…dating?"

"Sort of." She gave her a rundown of their "dates," and said they were meeting this coming Saturday, too. "I don't know what to do. I thought I would help him the one time then back away. I thought I could do that. But I can't."

"Or rather, you don't *want* to."

"Right. I don't want to." She pushed a piece of lettuce more securely under the bun and stared at it. "I don't know what to do."

"You can't just have fun with it? With him? He won't be your direct supervisor for much longer."

Which stung, too, Sara Beth thought. "But he's a doctor. And he's stayed single all these years. And he's absentminded, you know, which apparently has caused many of his relationships in the past to end. Or so he said. I would just be another in a string of forgettable women."

"You don't know that."

"Are you encouraging me toward him?"

"I'm not discouraging you." She smiled and waved. "He just spotted us. He's coming this way." They watched him walk over. "Hi, Ted."

"Lisa. Sara Beth. You didn't mention you were coming here tonight."

"I didn't know until the last minute," Sara Beth said. "Come here often?"

"My first time, actually. It's…loud."

She grinned. After all the quiet hours he spent in the lab, then in his otherwise empty loft, she could see why he would notice the noise even more than she did. "I recommend the burgers."

"Thanks."

"Who's the man with you?"

"An old friend, in town for the day. How're you, Lisa?"

Fascinating. Not only did he change the direction of the conversation, he didn't name his friend, nor bring him over for an introduction. Sara Beth wondered what Ted's well-mannered mother would think of that. Chance waved, but that was all.

"What is this? Institute night?" Lisa said, looking toward the front door. "Brother Derek just arrived."

Sara Beth couldn't imagine anyone more out of place, even more so than Ted. Derek had an air of entitlement about him. Fitting in wasn't something he did well.

He spotted them and headed toward them. Sara Beth

felt Lisa stiffen beside her. Considering how close Lisa had been to her big brother all her life, Sara Beth was surprised at how reluctant Lisa was to see him now. Because of the money problems Lisa had alluded to earlier? He was the CFO of the institute. He would know before anyone else if they were in trouble.

"Good evening, all," Derek said, and got lukewarm greetings in return. "I haven't seen you here before, Ted."

"My first time."

"Are you alone?"

Ted gestured toward where Chance and the other man sat. "I'm with friends."

Everyone looked that direction. Even from a distance, Sara Beth saw Ted's friend go rigid, his already intense expression turning icy. Derek's, too, Sara Beth noticed, then he pulled his cell phone out of his pocket and answered it. She hadn't heard it ring, but maybe it was on vibrate.

"My friend just canceled," he said, slipping his phone back in his pocket. "Good to see you, sister dear. We should have dinner sometime."

Lisa didn't say a word. He left, not stopping to say hello to Chance.

"That was strange," Sara Beth said.

Ted told them to enjoy their dinner and returned to his table. Sara Beth picked up her burger again then noticed that Lisa had shoved her plate away, her food not even half-eaten. She didn't usually waste food.

"I shouldn't have let you talk me into coming tonight, Sara Beth. I need to trust my instincts more."

"Who could've predicted that Derek would show up? And don't tell me this has nothing to do with him. You were fine until he came along." Her voice drifted off as Ted, Chance and the stranger got up from their table and went to the door. Ted lifted a hand toward her. "Getting even weirder," she said.

"I'd like to go, too."

Sara Beth wanted to talk more about Ted, about what she should do. If she could talk it through, she might get a better handle on her feelings before she and Ted spent another Saturday together. But even if she and Lisa stayed at the pub, Sara Beth probably couldn't get the help she needed. Not tonight, anyway. Lisa was too distracted.

"I'm sorry, Sara Beth. I'm not good company tonight. Oh, look. Carrie and Lorene just got here. They can take my place at the table."

"I don't want to stay without you. Just give me a couple of minutes to finish my dinner."

Carrie and Lorene, both institute employees, pulled up chairs and livened the conversation until Lisa and Sara Beth paid their bill, then Lisa drove Sara Beth home.

"Again, I apologize," Lisa said, double parking.

Sara Beth gave her a big hug. For a moment, Lisa leaned into it.

"Call me night or day," Sara Beth said. "We've been through a lot, you know?" Closer than sisters most of the time.

"I do know. Thanks. Keep me up-to-date about how it goes with Ted. You've been ready to settle down for a while now. Maybe he is, too."

"I think he's married to his work."

"I get the same impression. But that doesn't mean it's impossible."

"Maybe." Sara Beth opened the car door, then turned to look at her friend. "Night or day, Lisa."

She nodded.

Sara Beth spent what was left of the evening doing laundry, paying bills and making out a grocery list— mundane, mindless chores that allowed her thoughts to run freely, which only left her more confused. How could she fight her attraction to Ted? *Should* she? She admired so much about him. Respected his intelligence and dedication. And she'd spent a whole lot of time wondering what it would be like to kiss him, to touch him, to feel him touch her beyond the mostly accidental brushes so far.

As she was climbing into bed, her phone rang.

"I hope this isn't too late," Ted said.

"Not at all."

"I didn't want to bring up our personal lives at work."

"Okay." She prepared herself for the worst. He'd decided to keep his distance from her, keep their relationship business only. Or maybe Tricia had gotten to him. Or—

"I'd like to take you out to dinner on Saturday after we're done at the loft. As a thank-you. Would you like to go?"

"Yes." Maybe she should've hedged a little, but she was so relieved, the word just flew out.

"I could either take you home to change, or you could

bring clothes with you when I pick you up that morning. Whichever you're most comfortable with."

"Okay. Thanks."

A small pause, then, "You're probably wondering why we left Shots."

"A little."

"We decided it was too noisy."

"Really? I would've said it had to do with Derek."

Silence, then, "Yeah. I get tired of defending my research to him. I've said over and over that a practical treatment will take time. We're going to put a dent in it, I hope, then maybe another and another. One step at a time. Everyone needs to be realistic."

"You're right. Hopes are high."

"As are mine for that burger. I'll try another time, maybe, when there isn't a need for conversation."

"They make good fish and chips, too." She smoothed her blanket. "We left soon after you. It was a noisier-than-usual night."

A few beats passed. "I guess I'll see you in the morning, Sara Beth. Sleep well."

"Thanks. You, too." She pressed the off button then hugged the phone to her chest. She had a date with Ted Bonner. A real date, not a date of desperation, like the dinner with his parents, or a please-help-me-decorate date, but a get-dressed-up-and-go-to-dinner date.

And only three long days to decide whether to risk giving in to her feelings or ignore them.

Chapter Nine

Over the next few days, anticipation of her dinner with Ted replaced Sara Beth's letdown over not being allowed into the vault. Strangely, however, since he'd extended the invitation, they'd lost their ability to talk easily to each other.

Did he regret inviting her?

He'd picked her up on Saturday morning right on time. They'd shopped for hours, buying almost everything left on their list, once again having it all delivered the same day. She'd brought her change of clothes with her, not wanting him to have to drive her home, find parking and wait for her while she got ready.

After they'd hauled empty boxes and bags down to the trash, and before she got ready for dinner, they both sat on the sofa, their feet propped on the new coffee table, an oversize ottoman covered in a fabric that complemented the brown leather sofa. They'd finished hanging all of his art, had decided he would need a few more pieces, but only when he found something he loved. She was especially happy with his bedroom, not just the art, but the luxurious bedspread, in a gorgeous black and chocolate brown fabric that suited him exactly.

"Did I say how good you look in jeans?" she said, toasting him with her soda. He was wearing jeans and a white dress shirt with the sleeves rolled up. Not completely casual, but very sexy.

"You may have mentioned it a few times. I think I got the point, Sara Beth." He returned the toast. "We did well."

"You should throw a party."

"Why'd you have to go ruin my good mood?"

She laughed. "Most people have a housewarming, you know. You'll get a few plants, which you need, some bottles of good wine—"

"Which I also need," he interrupted.

"Right, because you can't afford to buy your own."

He grinned.

"And you'll get other stuff you'll never find a place for," she went on. "Can't mess with tradition. Plus, you'll make your mother happy."

"True. I'd make her happier if I announced I was engaged."

Conversation came to a halt. Sara Beth didn't squirm, but only because she made herself sit still. Ted, on the other hand, put his feet on the floor and took a long sip of soda.

"Sorry," he said after a minute.

"No problem. I think that point had already been established at your parents' anniversary party. So, have you seen Tricia since then?" She hoped she sounded really casual, as if his answer wasn't crucial to her well-being.

"We're having dinner tomorrow."

If the previous silence had been loud, this one was deafening.

"I seem to be making room in my mouth for both feet today. Would you accept it as a compliment that I don't have my usual self-censors up?"

She had to think about that. She could be flattered— or not. A man who was romantically interested probably wouldn't talk about taking another woman out to dinner.

"I guess not," he said. "I do apologize."

"Forget it. She's an old friend, and I'm not your girlfriend. It doesn't matter." Her words came out more harshly than she'd intended. She *had* begun to feel proprietary toward him. She'd had a hard time keeping her hands off him in the lab, and he'd often made excuses for getting close to her, bending over her shoulder to look at something on her monitor, when he could've just sat next to her.

More important, he didn't go off into Ted-world as frequently, but was usually aware she was in the same room.

So, she'd begun to hope. Now she knew she shouldn't.

"She really is just an old friend," he said. "There's nothing there."

"You don't have to explain anything to me, Ted." She stood. "I'll go change."

Her excitement about the evening dimmed. She'd needed the reminder about their different worlds, his being one in which Tricia fit. Plus, they had a history. Histories mattered. Being able to trace your family tree to the dark ages mattered to some people, and half of Sara Beth's branches were missing.

She undressed, then looked at her image in the mirror. *Okay, so a future with Ted is out of the question, but what about now? This moment?*

Sleeping with him—provided he was even interested—would break personal rules, including those drummed into her head all her life by her mother.

But what about the adventure?

Even that was coming to an end. His loft was decorated. The investigation would wrap up soon. They wouldn't be thrown together anymore, but would have to make a conscious decision to see each other. Would he? Did she want to wait to find out?

She figured she had the next couple of hours at dinner to decide.

The longest two hours in recent memory.

Ted took a swig of his Coke, finishing it off, trying to ignore the fact that Sara Beth O'Connell was standing naked in his bathroom, right next to his shower, a place comfortably big enough for two. He kept the picture of both of them showering together in his mind for a while, savoring it.

Then, resting his arms along the back of his sofa, he inspected his decorated space, appreciating it, already forgetting how barren it used to look. Not to mention he'd actually taken off two Saturdays in a row—although his situation at the lab had allowed for it, too. He and Chance had put together a product that might increase sperm count and motility, their goal for years now.

Time and testing would tell.

In the meantime, they would continue the research. There was still much to accomplish. Plus there was the investigation to complete, to clear the institute's name.

After which Sara Beth would return to her former duties.

No, not immediately. She was supposed to help him put together a best-practices manual, which would take a little while longer.

He'd come to enjoy having her around, her presence oddly calming—oddly, because she also excited him. Even Chance had commented that Ted had seemed more relaxed than he could remember. Except that Chance hadn't caught him staring at her, enjoying the way her braid lay along her spine, swinging as she moved. Or the curve of her rear when she bent over. Or the eye-catching bit of cleavage or lace when she wore V-necked sweaters, as she had today. Black sweater, her bra trimmed with black lace.

Black underwear, too? He'd bet on it.

"All yours."

Her voice shot into his fantasy like a fire-tipped arrow. *All yours.* She meant the bathroom, of course, but he considered a different meaning for a few seconds before turning toward her.

She wore another basic black dress, but this one fit like a second skin. It dipped low, exposing the high curves of her breasts and more than a little cleavage, a gold oval locket brushing her flesh, dipping between her breasts. Her eyes didn't shine with her usual good humor but with intensity—or maybe anticipation.

"You look beautiful," he said, which was an understatement.

She gave a small, playful curtsy, then sniffed her arm. "I smell like you, or rather your hand soap."

He went to her and lifted her arm until the scent reached him. He remembered the moment a week ago when he'd hugged her, and her nipples had turned hard, which he could see happening now, too. He hooked a finger around her locket, lifting it free, the back of his finger sliding along her upper breast. She held her breath, yet still her flesh quivered.

"Are there pictures inside?" he asked.

"My mom and me."

"May I see?"

She nodded.

Gauging his welcome, he let his hands just barely rest against her as he undid the latch and opened the locket. "You must've been a teenager."

"Yes. Fifteen."

He snapped it shut then didn't let go, his fingers itching to dip below her neckline, wishing he could fill his hands with her. "You haven't asked me not to touch you," he said, lifting his gaze to hers.

"No."

The breathless sound gave him a broader answer, the answer he wanted. "Tell you what. I'll go change and give you time to think. If you've tested the idea in your hand, and it still comes up positive…"

"This isn't science, Ted," she said, a small, nervous smile forming on her kissable lips.

"We work together."

"Not for much longer."

He stared at her mouth and the pale pink lipstick staining her lips, which parted invitingly. He bent low, touched his mouth to hers. Heat zapped his midsection and rocketed through him, the after-burn scorching him everywhere. He grabbed tight, pulled her against him, deepened the kiss, wanting all of her, everything she had to give.

She drew a quick breath, flattened her hands against him, pressed her forehead to his chest.

"I'm sorry." He moved back slightly, having registered the surprise in her face—or fear. He didn't know which. "Too much. Too soon. I'll give you some time." He turned around.

"Ted, wait."

He felt like a teenager about to be reprimanded.

"It's okay," she said, laying a hand on his arm.

Not a reprimand, after all. "I lost control."

"So?"

He faced her. The shock or fear, whatever it was, was gone. "I would've hauled you down to the sofa without thinking twice about it."

"Then stop thinking." She smiled, slow and steamy,

a Sara Beth he never would have anticipated. She was so…girl next door. Or so he'd thought.

"I'd prefer my bed," he said, thinking that far ahead.

She looped her arms around his neck and moved against him. "Me, too."

He almost thanked her. Then he scooped her up and carried her to his bed, standing her beside it. He inched her zipper down, the sound crackling with anticipation. Her dress dropped to the floor, blanketing their feet. He'd guessed right. All black undergarments, including garter belt and stockings. Her body was about as perfect as a woman's could be. "Look what you keep hidden under your scrubs. Is this what you wear to work?"

"I like the feel of silk and lace against my skin." She unbuttoned his shirt, pulled it loose and pressed her lips to his chest. "Mmm. This feels nice, too."

He unhooked her bra, slipped it down her then tossed it aside. He filled his hands with her breasts, ran his thumbs over her nipples. His mouth watered.

"Um, Ted?"

Don't make me stop now. Please don't. "Yeah?"

"You know those pocket protectors you wear at work?"

"Seriously? You're going to get after me about that now? Now?"

"Um, no." She laid her palms against his chest. His muscles twitched. "I'm hoping you have a different kind of pocket protector here at home. I can't tolerate the pill."

Was that all? He nudged her hair aside with his nose, dragged his lips down her neck, tasting her fragrant skin. "I was an Eagle Scout. What do you think?" He reached into his nightstand, pulled out a condom and flipped it onto a pillow.

"Got more than one?"

He laughed, shoved the bedding out of the way, then finished undressing. Lifting her in his arms, he laid her on the bed, landing on top of her, kissing her until she moaned, her lips soft and yielding, her mouth welcoming. He unwrapped the rest of her, revealing the gift of her body, tasting and savoring her as he went until she was naked and shaking. He didn't let her touch him, afraid everything would happen too fast. This was his present to himself. He intended to enjoy it. So he spent a lot of time swirling her nipples with his tongue, sucking them into his mouth, her back arching, sounds of pleasure coming from her throat. He moved down her body, teased her with long strokes of his tongue until she grabbed his hair and pulled him up, groaning as they kissed, wet and openmouthed, desire flowing from her.

He drew her hand to him finally, wrapped it around his erection and closed his eyes at the erotic sensation as she moved her hand up, down and around, gently. Too gently. He needed a faster rhythm, stronger motion. Completion.

He ripped open the condom, rolled it down, pulled her under him and plunged. Then he didn't move a muscle, but felt, just felt…

Sara Beth waited for him to move, the pressure inside her growing by the second.

"You're perfect," he whispered, gruff and low, sliding his hands under her, lifting her impossibly closer, their bodies fused. He moved just a little, creating a tiny bit of friction at the most responsive spot. Her world spun, pleasure burst inside her. She threw back her head, sounds coming out of her that she'd never heard before.

Then just when she was coming down, he moved, rhythmically, powerfully, and she was sent soaring again, beyond the realm of the first time, taking her to a place she wanted to stay forever....

Because she was falling in love with him. Falling for the ethical, cause-devoted, brilliant man who tried to conform to expectation but was his own man, nonetheless. No one could tell him what to do or how to live his life. He just lived it.

Sara Beth dug her fingers into his back as the realization struck her. How could she love him? It was too soon, too fast. Unrealistic.

Idiotic.

Desire was one thing, but love? No. She was just reacting to the best sex she'd ever had. He'd paid complete attention to her, just like he worked, single-minded, but this time devoted to the cause of giving her pleasure. Twice.

Just then he rolled to his side, wrapped her close and held her. No words. No kisses. Just the beat of his heart thundering in her ear, gradually slowing into a strong, steady beat.

"You okay?" he asked finally.

Okay? No, she wasn't okay. She was shell-shocked. Satisfied. Sated.

"Never better," she said.

"Same here. Best birthday ever."

She tipped back her head to make eye contact. He didn't look relaxed, but serious and tense. "Birthday? Why didn't you say so?"

"Because it's not important."

"I think it is. I love birthdays. I would've gotten you something special. Or baked you a cake with thirty-three candles to blow out."

"You gave me a gift already. As for the cake, I don't need to be reminded that time is passing by that fast."

He tucked her close again, his chin resting against her head. He'd started thinking about other things, she could tell. She just wished she knew what.

"I've never known anyone like you," he said finally. "Never had a...friend like you."

Friend. The word sounded like a death knell on the heels of her realizing she wanted more from him. Friend? What marked the difference for him between friend and girlfriend?

And, really, what made her think she felt more? The heat of the moment, probably. Best sex of her life, too.

Friend. That probably was a much truer definition.

"Same here," she said, feeling him tense up as he waited for her to say something in return. "I can't think of anyone else I could work and play with without problems occurring in at least one of the situations."

"I'll be right back." He rolled out of bed, disappeared into the bathroom.

Sara Beth untangled the sheet to cover herself, was just getting comfortable when he came walking back in all his naked glory. Yes, he was lean and lanky, but he didn't lack for muscles, either, and he had long, sturdy legs and a broad chest tapering to narrow hips. All that wonderful masculinity in one gorgeous package, one he knew how to use to bring unmatched pleasure.

He lifted the sheet and climbed in, settling on his side, resting his head on his hand, staring at her for so long she ran a hand over her mouth. "Do I have birthday cake on my face?"

He laughed. "You are a complete surprise, Sara Beth."

"In a good way?"

"In an exceptional way." He brushed her hair from her face. "I've been watching you for months. No, *admiring* you for months. I've listened to Chance praise your professionalism. I've seen you being competent yet kind. I know you have a depth of sympathy and empathy that make you a good nurse. When Lisa said you were going to be helping us, I was glad and relieved. Professional, competent, sympathetic and empathetic. That was good enough. But sexy, too? You're a fascinating woman."

Fascinating friend, you mean. And you have a date with an old girlfriend tomorrow night. "There's more to you than I first thought, too," she said, sidestepping the issue of Tricia. And parental wishes to procreate— with one of his own kind, Sara Beth was sure.

"So, size does matter?" His grin was wide, his eyes alight with humor.

"That falls into the category of bonus."

The phone rang. He ignored it, although he also

looked uncomfortable, since it would go to his answering machine, which she would also be able to hear.

"You can pick it up," she said, feeling sorry for him—until Tricia's voice came on the line, her nasally voice distinctive.

"Hey, Chip. Just wanted to send you birthday greetings on the actual day. I'm really looking forward to tomorrow. Your mom said you got your place decorated, so maybe I could meet you there and see it before we head out? We have lots of catching up to do—in more ways than one. Ciao."

Sara Beth pulled the sheet a little higher. Tricia's voice had a tantalizing edge to it, as if she had in mind an evening of unwrapping a special present of her own for him, too. It tarnished everything that had just happened with Ted.

She tried to keep her voice level. "Chip?"

"After the singing cartoon chipmunk, Theodore."

"Was that your nickname as a kid?" It sounded like a Boston royalty nickname—Chip, Muffy, Miffy, Trey.

Ted looked distinctly uncomfortable. "Not in general, no." He cupped her shoulder. "She's just a friend."

"Like me." She couldn't hold it in any longer. She didn't want to be just his friend, not if Tricia had the same significance. She started to climb out of bed, but he stopped her.

"You're more than that," he said.

"Am I? In what way?"

Confusion crossed his face. "I'm sleeping with you."

"Friends with benefits?" She hated that term. It

turned sex into something almost meaningless, just satisfying a physical need, nothing else.

"Works for me."

She'd gotten herself into this situation. He hadn't said he felt more for her, so she only had herself to blame.

The problem was, she was jealous of Tricia Trahearn. She'd never been jealous before—or had to share before. She didn't want to start now.

She made herself sound light and unconcerned. "So. Are we going to dinner? I'm starved." She didn't really want to sit across a table from him right now, either, but it was a better alternative to giving up more of herself to him without getting enough in return.

He was quiet for several seconds. "You're upset."

"I'm hungry." She got out of bed, uncomfortable at first, then deciding to let him see what he would be missing in the future—because she wasn't going to sleep with him again. No friends with benefits for her.

She had to dig through bedding to find all her clothes, then she dressed as he watched, feeling her cheeks heat up but ignoring it. She found the tote she'd brought, pulled out her brush and went into the bathroom, shutting the door. She leaned against the vanity, stared into the mirror, seeing splotches of color in her usually pale cheeks. Her lips were a little swollen from being kissed thoroughly and well.

She soaked a washcloth with cold water, pressed it to her face, her eyes stinging. *Idiot.* The word rang and rang in her head as she brushed her hair and fixed her makeup. Somehow she needed to find a way to smile, not to let him know how it mattered that he only considered her a friend. It wasn't his fault that her expectations were higher than his ability to meet.

She wasn't a match for him, anyway, their places in the world too vastly different from each other.

He was waiting in the living room, standing at his window, watching the lights. He turned. He'd dressed in his more typical dark slacks and white shirt, but also a muted tie. He still hadn't gotten his hair cut, and it curled over his collar. Tall, dark and gorgeous indeed.

He walked toward her, stopped a foot away, close enough to touch but not doing so. His eyes were filled with concern. She smiled. He really was a good person, which was why she'd fallen for him. But she couldn't make him feel the same as she did, no matter how much she wished it.

"I'm sorry," she said, needing the discomfort between them to end. "I was being prickly for no good reason. It all happened so suddenly, you know? I needed a few minutes to figure it out."

"You regret what happened?"

"No."

He hesitated. "Are you still hungry?"

She wasn't sure how to take that. Hungry for food or him? "Yes," she said, since both possibilities were true. Let him figure it out.

"Do you have all your stuff?"

She pointed toward the elevator, where her tote bag sat.

"Okay, then."

She didn't know what they would talk about over

dinner, but they managed to spend the next couple of hours doing just that, talking, finding ease with each other again. Then when they arrived at her house, he didn't argue with her when she said she didn't need him to walk her to her door.

He kissed her cheek before she got out of the car. "Thank you."

She didn't want clarification of what for. "You're welcome. I'll see you at work on Monday."

"Yeah."

"Good night, Ted."

"Good night."

As soon as she made it into her apartment, she turned on lights. Lots of lights. She had no intention of wallowing. She only hated admitting her mother was right. Now she would have to see Ted every day at work, knowing how it felt having him make love to her. Knowing her emotions were wrapped up in him, but not his in her.

She would recover. Time was her friend. Distance, too. They would stop working together directly soon.

But deep down she knew the memory of this night would stay close to her heart.

Chapter Ten

The next night, Ted watched Tricia wander around his loft, offering her opinion about every piece, recommending changes here and there. He hadn't let her meet him here, but picked her up and drove her to dinner at a restaurant she'd chosen, one where they'd run into several old friends. She'd paid for the meal, her birthday present, she'd said.

Some things just felt wrong to him, and having a woman pay for his meal was one of them, no matter how successful she was.

This felt wrong, too, having Tricia here in his space. Sara Beth's space. Sara Beth was the one to recommend the casual seating by the front window, a place he was drawn to more and more, where he could enjoy the view as he relaxed, morning or evening. Yet Tricia thought there should be a larger table, and seating for four, that the scale was somehow off.

Maybe it was. He had no idea about such things. But he liked the coziness of the two chairs, and a table small enough to hold only a couple of small plates and mugs. Tricia hadn't thought much of the throw laid across the bottom of his bed, declaring the faux fur passé.

Perhaps she was also right about that, but it felt luxurious under his fingers. Sara Beth had noticed how he had fingered it at the store and said he just had to have it. So now he did, and he didn't care whether it was passé or not. He had plans for it in front of the fireplace with a certain sexy girl-next-door type head nurse.

His bedroom walls were painted a deep, rich brown now, too, which felt strong and masculine to him, something else Tricia questioned the wisdom of.

"Aren't you going to offer me a nightcap?" she asked. She wore a dress as low cut as Sara Beth's the night before, except Tricia's was look-at-me purple.

"What's your pleasure? Coffee? Brandy? Wine?"

"Brandy, thanks." She eased onto a bar stool as Ted went behind the kitchen counter. "I had a good time tonight."

"Me, too," he said, meaning it. They'd taken a trip down memory lane. He'd forgotten some events, wanted to forget others, and could never forget some, as well. As the top two brainiacs in their high school, they'd shared a unique bond.

He passed her a small snifter, poured one for himself, but leaned against the kitchen counter rather than suggesting they sit in the living room.

She raised her glass to his, touched it briefly. "To old friends."

"I'll drink to that." They both took sips, looking at each other over the rims.

She cupped her glass with both hands. "Speaking of old friends, what do you hear from Rourke Devlin?"

Ted shrugged. "Rourke's got the world on a string. From humble beginnings to self-made billionaire. He always had the drive and talent to pull it off, although I never would've guessed he would succeed to the degree he has."

"He lives in New York, still?"

"A huge Park Avenue penthouse with views of Central Park and the Manhattan skyline."

"Has he been seeing anyone since his divorce?"

"I would guess the answer to that would be *plenty.* But we haven't discussed it. Why? Are you interested?"

"Maybe. My first choice seems to be taken."

Ted didn't respond immediately. "How do you know that?"

"You didn't touch me once tonight. I never caught you looking south of my face, either."

Given the fact he was a healthy male, he'd looked. He just hadn't wanted to take it further than that.

"What do your parents think of her?" she added into his silence, swirling her brandy slowly.

"It's not something I seek their opinion about."

"They've always had plans for you, you know. The only son, the golden boy."

"Did they say something to you?"

"About Sara Beth?" Tricia asked. "Not specifically. Just a general remark about how important roots are."

"I hear an echo from years gone by."

She laughed. "They mean well."

"No doubt. Shall I take you home?"

She made a point of looking at her watch, letting him know it was early still, only nine-thirty, then set her empty glass next to his barely touched one and picked up her evening bag. "I'd hoped for a different end to the evening."

"We had our day, Tricia."

"Yes, I suppose we did. So, how about sharing Rourke's phone number?"

He laughed as he walked her to the elevator. "He's not an Eagle Scout anymore."

"Meaning?"

"A man can't rise to the position he has without being…" The elevator door opened. He held it, letting her precede him.

"Ruthless?"

"That's part of it." He punched the garage button, giving *ruthless* a thought. "I just know he'd probably jeopardize your chances of rising to the Supreme Court."

"I'm not looking for matrimony, Chip. Just a little action. I have to be a lot more careful when I'm in my own town."

The elevator bounced to a stop. "Tell you what. I'll let him know you're interested."

"Never mind. I'm not sure my ego can take rejection from both of you."

He dropped her off at her parents' house a few minutes later. Without conscious thought he aimed his car toward Cambridge, making a deal with himself as he went. If he found a parking space within a block, he would call Sara Beth and ask if he could come up. If not, he would go back home. Leave it in the hands of fate.

As he neared her house he started looking, inching down the street, then beyond by one block, the parameters he'd set. No spaces anywhere.

He gripped the steering wheel. Okay. That was it, then. He made a right turn, then another, another, then one more, when he should've turned left, finding himself on the same route, and still no parking. He glanced at the dashboard clock. A little after ten. Too late to call, anyway.

Once again he made a right turn, another, one more. *Turn left. Go home....*

He turned right. A car pulled away from the curb in front of him. Fate, just a little delayed.

Ted nosed his car into the space and sat. And sat. He wasn't close enough to see if her lights were still on, but that alone wouldn't mean she didn't have company, either.

Or that she would welcome him. Things had ended on an iffy note last night.

At ten-fifteen Ted got out of his car and started walking. Her living room lights were out. He'd stalled too long.

Yet he kept on walking, not hesitating a step. He

rang the bell to her unit, waited what seemed like forever until the front door opened.

"Ted?"

She wore flannel pajamas with fire engines printed on the fabric, along with the words *hot stuff, sizzle* and *smokin'*. And teddy-bear slippers.

"Are you okay?" she asked, hugging herself against the cold.

"May I come in?"

"Why?"

"I'd like to clear the air."

She studied his face for what seemed like an hour then stepped back so that he could come inside. He signaled her to lead the way up the stairs. She smelled of toothpaste and soap.

"How was your date?" she asked as they crossed the threshold, her voice taut.

"On a scale of one to ten? A five." She didn't ask him to sit, which said a lot to him. "Are you wondering what I'd rate our date last night?" he asked.

"No."

He smiled. "Eleven."

"That's nice."

He would've laughed at how casually she said it, except she might not take what he had to say next seriously. "We left things up in the air last night, Sara Beth, and I wanted to be sure we're on the same page, so there's no confusion, no awkwardness at work tomorrow."

"About what?"

"We talked about being friends with benefits."

Her jaw clenched. "*You* talked about it."

"Yes, I realized later that you hadn't weighed in on it at all."

"Because I'm not interested."

"In the friends part, or the benefits part?"

She crossed her arms. "The combination."

He pondered that. "So, we could be friends. Or we could be lovers. Those are the choices?"

"I didn't mean it that way."

Because he couldn't resist, he swirled a lock of her soft hair with his finger, then tucked it behind her ear. "How did you mean it, Sara Beth?"

"I like both aspects. I just don't like the label, friends with benefits. It implies a freedom to have *other* friends with benefits. When I'm with someone, I'm exclusive."

"I didn't sleep with Tricia." He ran his finger around her ear, heard her breath catch. Encouraged, he rubbed the lobe with his fingers.

"Did she offer?" Sara Beth asked. When he didn't reply, she said, "She did. I knew it."

"What difference does it make? We didn't."

She pushed his hand away. "Why not? She's so right for you. You have all that history. You fit into each other's lives."

There were so many reasons, ones that were becoming clearer to him by the minute as she stood there in her pajamas and teddy-bear slippers looking once again like the girl next door. He knew when the pajamas were off, she was a fantasy come to life.

"She doesn't make me laugh, Sara Beth," he said. "I don't make her laugh."

Her big brown eyes opened wide. "That's important to you?"

"Isn't it to you?"

"Well, yes, but—"

"And I don't watch her walk away, wanting to put my hands on her."

"You do that? Watch me like that? Want me like that?" Her voice had gone softer, and a little breathless.

"For months. And since you started working in the same room? It's been hell."

"I never would've guessed."

"I'm surprised you didn't catch me eyeing you with lust a hundred times, even in your scrubs. I want you, Sara Beth. Only you." He reached for her. "Come to bed with me."

"The couch is closer," she said, diving for him. At first he tried to slow her down, then he caught up and took over, undressing both of them in a rush of unbuttoning, unzipping, tugging and tossing. His memories of last night were shoved aside, replaced by this incredibly passionate, sexy, demanding version of the endlessly complex Sara Beth.

He took the few steps to her sofa, pulling her down with him, letting her straddle him, lifting her hair over her shoulders so that he could see all of her.

"You're all I've thought about all day long," she said, kissing him.

"Same for me." Every minute. Relived every moment of the night before, the urge to have her again all consuming.

"Good. I wanted you to be as tortured as I was," she said against his mouth.

"Wish granted."

He filled his hands with her breasts, savored their taste and texture until she dropped her head onto his shoulder.

"Hurry. Please hurry," she said, demand and need melding in her voice.

He found home with her as she sank onto him, then arched back, holding that pose, agony and ecstasy on her face, driving him over the brink, as well. She made glorious sounds, moved in a rhythm he helped establish and maintain, and exploded with a climax that came fast and loud. His followed, held, lingered…then eased, but slowly, the sensation lasting, fulfilling.

She fell against him, panting, her face pressed to his shoulder. "That was phenomenal," she said, breathing hard.

"Yeah."

A few seconds later she went rigid.

"What's wrong?" he asked, sure that something was.

She sat up, her skin gone pale, her eyes deep and dark. "No pocket protector."

He swallowed. "What's the timing like?"

"I have to look on my calendar. Because I'm not on the pill, it's not regular. In fact, it's very irregular."

She started to move off him. He cupped her arms, keeping her there. "The chances are slim."

"I know."

He was a doctor. He felt he had to bring up a possibility. "There's the morning-after pill...."

She shook her head, adamantly. "I can't. Is that what you want?"

He held her hands tightly. "I have spent my career trying to find ways to help people have children. No, it's not what I want. We'll cross that bridge if we come to it, okay?"

"Yeah."

"In the meantime, we'll make sure we use condoms. No sense tempting fate."

Fate. He'd left it to fate earlier as to whether or not he would see her tonight. And fate had seemed to put them in a situation where they hadn't been careful. He was always careful. He was pretty sure she was, too.

She finger-combed his hair, then locked her hands behind his neck. "Would you like to stay the night?" she asked, not looking completely sure of herself, or his answer.

"Do you have pocket protectors?"

She smiled, slow and sexy. "I'm pretty sure I do," she said. "If not, we can get creative."

"What do you say we get creative, with or without?" He kissed her, was relieved when she relaxed into him. "How big is your bed?" he asked.

"We'll both fit, provided I sleep on top of you."

Her sense of humor had returned—or had it? "Are you serious?"

She laughed. "It's queen size. I realize you're a king-size man—in more ways than one—but I think we'll fit okay." She wiggled her brows suggestively.

"Let's go give it a try."

"Eat my dust, Teddy Bear."

He caught up with her at her bedroom door and scooped her into his arms. They landed on the bed together.

"That was a quick recovery," she said, her eyes sparkling.

"I aim to please."

"Yeah? Show me."

He brushed his lips against hers. "It'll be my pleasure."

Chapter Eleven

Sara Beth gripped the lab telephone a little tighter. "Dr. Bonner is in a meeting, Ms. Goodheart."

"I told his mother that, Ms. McConnell. As I said, she asked if you were available until he's free." The efficient, professional, fifty-something administrative assistant who acted as the receptionist for the Armstrong Fertility Institute, Wilma Goodheart, had worked there longer than anyone, now that Sara Beth's mother had retired. She never gossiped, never called people by their first name, nor did she wear anything other than white button-down shirts and a gray or navy blue skirt. And she was one of the warmest people Sara Beth knew.

"I have no idea how long Dr. Bonner will be tied up,"

Sara Beth said. *And I don't want to entertain his mother for an hour.*

"She says they're meeting for lunch."

Sara Beth glanced at her watch. Almost noon. She shouldn't have to be alone with Penny Bonner for long....

Provided Ted remembered his mother was coming.

"Okay. I'll be right out," Sara Beth said into the phone. She left the lab, smoothed her hair and headed to the reception area.

It was Friday. Six days ago she and Ted had become lovers, exclusively as of Sunday, when he'd spent the night. On Monday they decided to sleep at their own houses, because he had to get up very early to meet someone before work. But by nine o'clock he'd showed up on her doorstep, hauled her to bed, then stayed until dawn, leaving her still cozy under the covers, her body aching pleasantly. They hadn't spent a night apart since, although they arrived at work separately so that no one would know.

Sara Beth didn't have any illusions. *Exclusive* didn't mean forever. It just meant for the moment. Until they were done. Or, according to Ted, until he forgot about her often enough that she gave up on him. He didn't understand that she admired him, that his single-minded dedication to his work was an appealing trait to her, especially since when he got single-minded about making love with her, she reaped the benefits of being the sole focus of his attention.

She entered the lobby as someone pushed open the heavy front door—Dr. Armstrong's wife, Emily Stanton

Armstrong. Sara Beth had been close to Mrs. Armstrong for many years, but then something had changed when Sara Beth was a teenager. Now Emily seemed to merely tolerate Sara Beth because she was Lisa's best friend, but Sara Beth hadn't been to the Armstrong home since Lisa first went off to college ten years ago.

"Hello, Mrs. Armstrong," Sara Beth said. "It's nice to see you again."

"Sara Beth."

"Emily!" Penny Bonner got up from the sofa and headed toward Emily Armstrong, her arms extended.

Panic whipped through Sara Beth. What if Ted's mother said something about him dating Sara Beth? Even Lisa didn't know they were sleeping together.

"Why, Penny, how wonderful you look." They exchanged polite hugs.

"I could say the same of you. Very rested."

"Isn't it amazing what a vacation will do? We went to Greece. To Mykonos, actually. We got home last night."

"How wonderful! I do adore that island. And that must mean that Gerald is doing well."

"I traveled with my sister. Gerald couldn't manage a trip like that anymore. Too much walking. He's nearing his eightieth birthday, you know."

Sara Beth felt like a third wheel as the two women, obviously old acquaintances, chatted. She also didn't want to excuse herself, in case she needed to interrupt.

"Please excuse my rudeness, Sara Beth," Penny said finally. "I haven't seen Emily in ages."

"It's fine." As long as she could monitor it.

"I'm meeting my daughter for lunch, anyway," Emily said to Penny. "She hates it when I'm late. Give my regards to Brant, my dear."

"And mine to Gerald."

"Of course. Sara Beth," Emily said in farewell, not making eye contact before she swept out of the room.

"We've served together on several committees and boards through the years," Penny said.

"Her daughter Lisa is my best friend." Sara Beth wondered if that would give her credibility with Ted's mother, let her think Sara Beth wasn't untested in their stratosphere. She'd been to formal parties at the Armstrong house and knew what to expect—and what was expected of her.

Penny leaned close. "I guess Greece is the place to go for face-lifts now."

Sara Beth tried not to smile too much at the catty remark. She'd noticed the difference in Emily, too. However, she didn't dare make a comment that could come back to haunt her. "Did you want company while you wait for Ted?"

"I'd like that, yes, and the chance to get to know you a little better. Do you mind if we wait here? I know places like employee lounges are usually busy this time of day."

"The lobby's fine." Sara Beth let her lead the way to her choice of seating, a small sofa by the front window. "I'm sorry I can't tell you when Ted's meeting might be over." She wondered if she should have Ms. Goodheart get a message to Ted, to remind him of his lunch date.

Since he hadn't told Sara Beth about it, she wondered if he remembered it himself.

"My son has been elusive since Valentine's Day." Penny's gaze was direct and only slightly accusatory, but Sara Beth didn't feel responsible for Ted's lack of contact with his parents.

"He's doing such important work." She was uncomfortable calling the woman Penny, so she didn't call her anything. "He works long days. And in his little bit of free time, he's been furnishing his loft." *Which should make you happy.*

"How long does it take to call his mother? I had to catch him by e-mail to arrange this lunch today." She settled back. "So, he's well?"

"Yes, very well."

"And his loft looks presentable, finally?"

"It looks like him." Sara Beth smiled at the thought. "Masculine, stylish, contemporary."

"Stylish?" She looked doubtful.

"He has his own style. It's represented in what he chose as furnishings. And he has some truly amazing art pieces. He said he learned about art from you."

"Did he? Sometimes one wonders what one's children take away from childhood." She looked pleased. "I suppose I'll have to drop by sometime and see for myself, since he hasn't extended an invitation."

"I think you'll like it." Sara Beth didn't know if he was going to throw a housewarming party as she'd suggested, so she didn't bring it up. His relationship with his mother was his business.

"I suppose you stay in touch with your mother. Daughters tend to be better at that than sons."

"I'm close to my mom." In this case, it was the mother who was doing the avoiding instead of the child. Sara Beth hadn't heard from her since her text message a week ago saying she was staying for another week. She should be back tomorrow, unless she decided to stay even longer.

"What does she think of Ted?"

"Actually, they haven't met. Mom's been out of town. You know," Sara Beth said, lowering her voice, "Ted and I haven't gone public. Since we work for the same company, we want to keep it quiet. I'm sure you understand."

"That makes good sense. Why make things potentially uncomfortable for others? Ted has always been aware of propriety."

And how would you feel if your model-of-propriety son found himself about to be a father? Sara Beth tried to ignore the possibility, but it simmered in her mind at times.

The lobby door opened and a woman entered. Wilma Goodheart smiled and raced around her desk to hug the new arrival.

"It's Mother's Day at the institute," Sara Beth murmured, amazed. "That would be my mom," she said to Penny.

"Well, how nice. We get to meet." She stood, then waited for Sara Beth to do the same.

The way this was going, Ted would probably show up—

Yep. Right on schedule. He walked into the lobby, a pink message slip in his hand. Ms. Goodheart must have sent a note to say his mother was here.

Since Sara Beth was the common denominator of the group, she made the introductions, although she moved everyone away from the reception desk. She was grateful that no one suggested they all have lunch together. Small blessings.

Ted sent her a woe-is-me look as he left the building with his mother. Sara Beth tried not to laugh.

She finally hugged her mother, welcoming her home. "You look rested, Mom. And more tan than I can remember you letting yourself get. I guess I don't need to ask if you enjoyed yourself."

"I had a wonderful time. I'd go right back tomorrow."

"Let's have lunch. You can tell me all about it," Sara Beth offered.

"It'll have to wait. Wilma and I are going out. What's your schedule for the weekend?"

"Busy. Full." She and Ted planned a drive to the shore, were going to stay overnight, be out where they wouldn't run into people they knew. "Tuesday, as usual, then?"

"That's fine." She bent close to Sara Beth. "Are you and Ted an item now? You and his mother were huddled awfully close."

"I've seen him a few times. We're not being open about it, so don't talk to Ms. Goodheart about it, okay?"

Grace raised a hand as if swearing to it. "But remember this, Sara Beth. If you can't be public about a relationship, something's not right about it. It's an additional stress, and it can lead to arguments and hurt feelings. Be careful, okay? Please, sweetheart. Guard your heart."

Sara Beth hugged her mother, whose cautionary words rang true, unfortunately. Secrets weren't good, and eventually were exposed. "Thanks, Mom. I'll be careful."

Although it was hard to guard her heart when it was already being held captive, even if its captor didn't realize it…

Sara Beth went for a walk during her lunch hour, needing to be alone and away from the institute. It was nearly spring. Green was beginning to be a dominant color after the drab browns and grays of winter, and was always a welcome sight. Rebirth. New beginnings. Yes, spring had always appealed to her.

And now that'd she'd resigned herself to never seeing her mother's file, she could have an especially good new beginning this season, a truly fresh start. She would never know her father, but she knew herself. Liked herself. That counted for a lot.

Ted was already in the lab working when Sara Beth returned. So was Chance. They acknowledged her but didn't stop their discussion, which was riddled with scientific lingo she couldn't hear well enough to make sense of. She finished the box of materials Ted had brought up the day before and needed more.

She waited for a good time to interrupt, then suddenly Ted left the room.

"Wait," she called out. "I need—" But the door shut, cutting off her words.

Chance met her gaze. "He'll be back. He's in one of

his zones and, frankly, I don't want to break into his thoughts. He's onto something. What is it you need?"

"Files. I'm not authorized to access the vault."

"I forgot. Why not, anyway?"

"I don't know. It wasn't something I'd ever had to do before, so it'd never concerned me."

Chance picked up the phone and dialed. "Lisa, it's Chance. Can I get authorization for Sara Beth to get files from the vault?... Right now.... Okay. How about temporary access?... Thanks." He hung up, then looked at his pager, which had gone off. "She'll meet you there. One time only, at least for now, so grab a couple of boxes while you're at it. I've got to get to the clinic."

It would be a special kind of torture, Sara Beth decided, being allowed in the vault while accompanied by a witness. Torture, and a test of her newfound sense of peace at having come to terms with never seeing her mother's file. Still, her legs were unsteady as she took the stairs down to the basement, carrying the box of files she'd just finished. She stumbled twice, her heart pounding so hard she couldn't hear anything but the thundering beat.

Lisa was right behind her.

"This place has always creeped me out," Lisa said.

"More lights would be a plus."

"Maybe. It's just old and scary." She slid her ID in the slot and pulled the steel door open. "Need some help?" Lisa asked.

Sara Beth's stomach churned as she went inside. She looked at the dates on the side of the box. "I need to refile these and fill up a couple more boxes from the next sequential dates."

Because the vault had previously been a panic room before the institute was rebuilt, it still contained a sofa and chair, as well as a bathroom. File storage was a room beyond the furnishings, out of direct sight. She and Lisa located where the folders belonged and returned them.

"Let's hurry. I hate being down here," Lisa said, shoving the empty box close to Sara Beth and grabbing another one.

A piece of her mourned the lost opportunity. She couldn't even manage a smile to soothe Lisa's fear of the dark. They filled the boxes without conversation between them, a rarity.

"Need some help?" Ted came into the room, making it seem half its size.

"Yes." Lisa headed out the door, calling back to Ted, "You can lock up. I'm outta here."

Her footsteps echoed as she ran up the stairs.

"Alone at last," he said, slipping his arms around Sara Beth, bending to kiss her. "I've been wanting to do this all day."

She couldn't kiss him. She couldn't even move. With Lisa gone, could she ask Ted for his help? Ask him to do something unethical? He'd found a six-dollar error on a furniture bill totaling thousands and had insisted on paying it. He'd reached the highest level of achievement the Boy Scouts had.

Everything he said and did advertised him as a highly

principled, ethical man. No, she couldn't ask him, couldn't back him into a corner like that. He would have to turn her down.

So she hugged him instead, then she did the only thing she could.

"Would you mind taking that box to the lab," she asked him, "while I finish packing this one?"

"I can carry two boxes, Sara Beth." He flexed his muscles and grinned.

She almost sighed. Apparently it just wasn't meant to be.

She gave it one last shot. "I think I'll pack four boxes. Then neither of us will have to come back down for a while."

"If ever," he said, sliding the last files into a box as she passed them to him. "I figure we'll have all the statistics we need by then." He hefted both boxes. "I'll be back."

A five-minute window of opportunity opened up for Sara Beth.

Not enough time to debate what to do. Only time enough for one thing—action.

Chapter Twelve

"Are you sure?" Lisa asked Ted in a closed-door meeting in Derek's office almost a week later. Chance leaned against a file cabinet. Paul paced. Lisa and Ted sat in visitor's chairs across from Derek's desk.

"Positive," Ted said.

"You have proof?"

"In the report I just handed you are statistics confirming that the institute has had a three-year run of above-average numbers of multiple births, enough to be suspicious that too many embryos were implanted. However, we also found similar statistics twice before in the institute's history, or at least in the past twenty years, which is as far back as we went for now. We believe in each case that it was purely happenstance. No one breached protocols."

"I told you," Derek said smugly. "We can use this information to our benefit right now. Let it be known that our in vitro procedures have a higher-than-average success rate. Business will boom."

Ted disliked Derek more each day, had come to resent the way he stopped by the lab almost daily, asking for a full accounting on the day's work, as if Ted and Chance were shirking their duties. They had decided not to tell Derek about their trial study until preliminary results were in.

"Just don't guarantee anything," Chance cautioned Derek. "As Ted said, it's happened before. Following that logic, it's likely to ease off, too."

Ted agreed. "What's important for the moment is that we found incomplete reporting of critical statistics. Sara Beth has done a thorough job of compiling the information and updating it into the new computer system. You'll be able to pull out any statistic you need, should anyone question the institute again."

"I can't tell you how grateful I am," Lisa said, then looked at her chief-of-staff brother, Paul. "It was hard having that shadow hanging over us."

"Yes, let me add my thanks," Paul said, something Derek hadn't bothered to do. "I think Lisa talked to you about writing a best-practices manual of lab protocols? It will be a required checklist that everyone will adhere to and enter into the computer. How long do you think that would take?"

"A week or so," Ted said. When they were finished with it, Sara Beth would return to her regular duties. He wouldn't get to turn his head and see her anytime he wanted. Couldn't watch her stretch out the kinks after an hour in front of the computer.

Or watch her stare into space now and then, unfocused. Was she pregnant and hadn't told him yet?

He thought back. She'd been distracted for almost a week—since the day they'd brought up the last boxes from the vault, actually. Their weekend at the shore hadn't been as relaxing as it should've been, even though they'd had all the privacy they'd sought.

"We need to bring Ramona in on this," Derek was saying. "Have her come up with a PR plan to let people know that the Armstrong Fertility Institute is seeing such great success. This is a good time for a push."

Paul nodded in agreement. Ted had met Paul's fiancée, Ramona, a few times and liked her. She had a good head on her shoulders and was an excellent strategist. Once a reporter, the institute had hired her as their public relations strategist.

"Let's talk to her together," Paul said finally, then glanced at his watch. "Thank you all again for your hard work to clear up this problem. I hope we can move forward now without distraction."

Ted and Chance walked down the hall to the lab.

"I don't suppose this means the end of Derek's visits to the lab," Chance muttered.

"I doubt it. He's always seemed more interested in our research than the disproportionate number of births.

I don't understand why he wasn't worried about that. The institute stood to lose a lot of money if, in fact, we had been implanting too many embryos, thus exaggerating results."

"I agree. The institute stands to pull in a hell of a lot of more money if our research yields results. And the sky's the limit if we can get beyond elevating sperm count and motility."

"He does seem interested more in dollars than reputation, doesn't he?" Ted mused. "I guess you don't become CFO without money being the main focus of your thinking."

"Speaking of the main focus of your thinking," Chase said. "You and nurse Sara Beth seem to have become...close."

Ted had promised Sara Beth he wouldn't talk to anyone about her, and he'd agreed. "I like her. It's been nice having her around. Breaks up the tedium when you're not there."

"Breaks up the tedium? Right." Chance laughed. "You're not fooling anyone."

Were they that obvious? Or had someone seen them together away from the office?

"You watch her with the same intensity as you conduct a tricky experiment. I think when you've finished writing the manual and she comes back to work with me, you should ask her out. I'm sure she would say yes."

Ted relaxed. "Maybe."

They went into the lab, finding it empty, except for a note from Sara Beth, telling him to call her when he wanted to start working on the manual, which he did right away.

He and Chance had barely gotten their computers up and running when the door opened, but Lisa came in, not Sara Beth.

"We have a problem," she said, handing them a sheet of paper bearing the Breyer Medical Center letterhead.

Before the door shut, Sara Beth arrived and said a happy good morning.

"Would you mind coming back in about fifteen minutes, please?" Lisa said to her.

"She can stay," Ted said as Chance grabbed the letter and swore.

"What's going on?" Sara Beth asked, coming closer, her gaze moving from person to person then staying on Ted.

"Our former employer is accusing us of unethical behavior regarding funding issues during our years there," Ted explained.

"No way," Sara Beth said. "No possible way."

"I appreciate your faith, but the burden of proof will be ours," Ted informed.

Sara Beth put a hand on Ted's. "You are the most ethical man on the planet. There's no way you've done anything wrong."

Guilt took a bite out of Ted. By not telling Derek or Paul that he and Chance had entered into a trial study with one subject, they weren't being forthcoming. And if a best-practices protocol manual had been in place a week ago, Ted couldn't have justified the secretive project.

"Are we ever going to be allowed to just do our jobs?" Chance asked, frustration in his voice. He threw the paper onto the lab counter and walked away to look out the window at the parking lot. "Ted and I came here to get away from the bureaucracy that Breyer burdened us with, constantly tying our hands. We've already made progress here that would've taken us years had we stayed there."

"What do they want?" Sara Beth asked.

"They say we recruited and used funds dishonestly," Ted answered. "That we promised impossible results."

"Can you think of anything they might have that they could use against you?" Lisa asked.

Ted shook his head as Chance almost shouted, "No. Nothing. We tried to do what we'd been hired to do. Even that was a daily uphill battle. We had to write our own grants, meet with potential investors, beat the drum. We were spending most of our time raising funds. It's no wonder we couldn't accomplish anything of value."

"Then it sounds like sour grapes to me," Lisa said. "When you left, their funds dried up."

"Did you keep copies of all the funding we got there?" Chance asked Ted.

"It's all on my home computer."

"I can't cancel my appointments today," Chance said. "But let's meet at your place tonight and go over it."

"Okay. If Lisa's right, and they're just trying to ruin our reputation, then we need to fight fire with fire. Let's ask Ramona to help, too. We could use a spin doctor's opinion."

Chance came back to the table. "If push comes to

shove, Ted and I know some things that Breyer wouldn't want made public."

Ted shifted uncomfortably. Yes, they knew secrets, which was one of the reasons why they'd left. They hadn't agreed with Breyer's methods all the time. "I hope it doesn't come to that," Ted said. "I don't want to be associated with dragging Breyer's name through the mud, either."

"The last thing we need is a loss of funding," Lisa said, her jaw tight. "I'll talk to Paul and Ramona. Um, I'd like to keep Derek out of the loop for a couple of days. See what we can come up with first." She looked at Chance, then Ted.

"No problem," Ted said.

Chance raised a hand in agreement.

"All right. Give me a call at home tonight after you've taken a look at your records." She walked out.

Chance swiped the accusatory letter from the counter, swearing as it drifted to the floor. "We left there to get away from chaos. Since then we've dealt with one problem after another. When will it end?"

He yanked open the door and left, angry and frustrated. Ted felt exactly the same. He just tended to internalize his emotions more.

"One scandal door closes and another one opens," he said to Sara Beth.

"You'll be cleared."

"It may not matter. Tarnished reputations are hard to polish." Like Chase, he was tired of the upheavals. "I've never been one to have secrets, Sara Beth."

Her sympathetic expression became guarded. "Are you still talking about your work?"

He shook his head.

"You want to go public about us," she said, not as a question, already knowing the answer.

"Not this second, but as soon as you stop working for me."

"Why?"

"Because right now I'd really like to hold you, and I can't do that. Anyone could walk by."

"There's always the supply closet."

Her response was so quick and unexpected, he laughed, then he hauled her to the closet, shut them inside and held her, just held her, until his anger dispersed, replaced with need for her, the incredible Sara Beth O'Connell, one of the kindest, most beautiful women he'd ever met.

He didn't want to keep her a secret anymore.

In the dark, he found her mouth with his, the taste of her familiar now, yet always arousing and exciting. They rarely spent a night apart, often talking into the late hours before falling asleep, her head on his shoulder, his arm around her, hers across his chest, then waking up in the morning with her wrapped in his arms.

One thing they'd avoided talking about was the possibility she could be pregnant. How long could they pretend not to notice?

"We'll go public," he said against her lips.

"We'll talk about it."

"Ted?" Derek's voice reached them inside the closet. They went utterly still. Sara Beth pressed her face to

Ted's chest. Her shoulders shook. Laughing? Seriously? She was the one who was so worried about going public, and she was laughing?

"Where could he have gone?" Derek said, his voice fading, then silence.

After a few seconds, Ted turned the knob slowly and peeked out. The room was empty. "Hurry up," he said, patting Sara Beth on the backside.

She laughed and scurried out just as Derek looked through the window and frowned. "Uh-oh," she said when Derek opened the door.

"Where were you? I was just here."

"Restroom," Ted and Sara Beth said simultaneously. He didn't dare look at her.

She headed to the door, not making eye contact, either. "I'll arrange my schedule so that we can start on the manual tomorrow, Dr. Bonner," she said.

"That'd be great, Ms. O'Connell, thanks." He looked down for a second to smooth his expression, and spotted the letter from the Breyer Medical Center lying on the floor, face up. Had Derek seen it when he'd been in a few minutes earlier? Ted figured him for a good poker player. If he'd read it, he would probably wait to see how long Ted took to tell him.

He scooped it up, folded it and stuck it in his back pocket. "What can I do for you, Derek?"

He didn't answer immediately. "I realized I hadn't thanked you for the work you did on the stats. Good job."

Ted figured Derek called it a good job because it had turned out well. If it hadn't...

"All I did was compile and run the numbers. But I'm glad it's over." He grabbed his lab coat from the coat rack near Sara Beth's desk. The room seemed empty without her. "Anything else?" Ted asked, waiting for the ax to fall.

"Just wanted an update."

"Nothing's changed since yesterday. When there's something to report, I will."

"I know you think I'm pushing too hard. But just word of the possibility we're close to a treatment would sustain us for now."

"Sustain us for now?" Ted repeated. "Is there a problem with keeping the research going?"

Derek shifted a little. "The program is expensive. Setting up the lab to your specifications was costly. Your salaries. So far, there haven't been any returns."

"That's the burden of research." What was going on? Was Derek saying the institute was having financial problems?

"I realize that. We just have to hope there are no more rumors or scandals. We had some close calls."

Ted nodded. Lisa had asked him to keep quiet, so he would, for now—and because he didn't trust Derek himself.

After Derek left, Sara Beth quietly slipped in.

He smiled. "The coast is clear." *Except Derek may have read the letter.*

"So, everything is okay?"

"I wouldn't go that far. But we'll have to skip seeing each other tonight. Chance and I may pull an all-nighter trying to figure this out."

"I'll try to hook up with my mom, since she canceled on me last night."

"Call me when you're getting off the bus."

She cocked her head. "How will you explain that to Chance?"

"I'll figure out something. Have a nice time with your mom."

"Thanks. I'll miss you."

He didn't say anything in return. He probably should, because he would miss her, for sure, but his confusion over her unwillingness to let their relationship be public held him back. Maybe she saw what they had as temporary. "Talk to you later," he said.

A little light went out of her eyes. He was sorry for that, but it was the best he could do for now.

Chapter Thirteen

"You're different, Mom," Sara Beth said as they lingered that night over dessert, apple tarts with cinnamon ice cream. The restaurant was one of her favorites, a small café that offered comfort food with a twist. For dinner she'd had chicken and dumplings, prepared with a delicate touch and fresh herbs. "Are you sure you don't have a man in your life?"

"I'm sure." Grace sipped her coffee, eyeing Sara Beth over the rim. "I retired months ago, but I hadn't gotten the hang of it yet. Now I have."

"Shouldn't that mean you'd be more relaxed? Because you're not. In fact, you're edgier. And you're not being forthcoming about your trip."

"There's just so little to tell, sweetheart. I didn't do much but read, go for walks, eat and sleep."

"You didn't take any tours? Didn't see the Mayan ruins? And where are your photographs? You always took a ton of pictures wherever we went."

"I was recording your life, Sara Beth. Hence, the many scrapbooks of years gone by. And you haven't said a word about Dr. Bonner."

"There's just so little to tell." Sara Beth flashed a smile.

"Touché."

For almost a week Sara Beth had lived with what she'd done, taking advantage of the unexpected opportunity in the vault to look for her mother's file. And for almost a week she'd lived with the results, not telling anyone that she'd looked—and discovered it was missing. Ted had noticed there was something wrong. She'd denied it.

But she also knew she would never come to terms with it unless she talked to her mother.

Sara Beth's heart lodged in her throat at the thought of asking, but she had to know. "Why is your file not in the vault?" Sara Beth blurted out, the words almost choking her.

For a long time, Grace said nothing. Then, finally, "It took you a long time to look. You've worked there for twelve years, six years full-time."

Which was no answer. Sara Beth's anxiety about asking turned to frustration—again. "Because I wanted you to be the one to tell me."

"Tell you what?"

"Who my father is."

"I've told you all your life."

"An anonymous donor." Sara Beth shoved her dessert away, unfinished. "But there's no record of your procedure, not even someone using an alias that came close to matching you, either."

"Think about that for a moment. I worked there for over thirty years. A lot of people had access to patient files."

"Meaning you removed it so that no one would know?"

"Everyone knew I'd gotten pregnant with help from the institute. But the details weren't—and aren't—anyone else's business."

"I don't count?"

Grace sat back. "What would you do with that information, if you had it?"

"I don't know. I just have a need to know where I came from. I feel like half of me is missing. Or a third," she said, correcting herself. "I know you, and I know myself. I'd like to know the missing link. Do I have siblings? What about a health history?" *Would he have brought me a Valentine if he'd known about me?*

"Many of the donors all those years ago were college students, Sara Beth, who were in it for the money. They were able to walk away without feeling any attachment for a child who might come of that generous donation. Do you think it would matter now, after all this time?"

"It could, perhaps even more so. Maybe he never had other children. Or whatever the reasons might be. I could contact him through an intermediary. If he wants to be left alone, I would respect that."

Their server approached, a reminder that they were in public. They paid their bill then left the café, heading back to Grace's house and the bus stop nearby.

"Let me think about it, okay, sweetheart?"

It was the first time her mother had dangled any kind of carrot in front of her. What could she say? It wasn't the right time to keep pushing. "Thank you."

Rain began to fall, light but steady, putting an end to their conversation as they each opened an umbrella, creating distance between them. They reached the bus stop.

"You don't need to wait with me in the rain, Mom. Go on inside."

"I'm not made of sugar."

Sara Beth laughed. "No, you're not. Neither am I, in large part because you made me that way. Thanks for being such a good life coach."

"I would say you're welcome, except I haven't entirely succeeded."

"I think I turned out okay."

"Despite my many warnings, you've fallen in love with a doctor, and one you work with, at that."

"I haven't—"

"Oh, sweetheart. You have. Do you think I don't know your every expression? That it isn't always what you say but what you don't say that speaks the loudest? You haven't volunteered a word about him all night."

Sara Beth could feel herself closing up. "Because I know how you feel about him. It. The situation itself."

"For good reasons. I was a nurse for a long time. I've

seen it happen again and again. It's one of the oldest professional fantasies in the world—nurse falls for doctor. Do you know how seldom it works out?"

"I'm having fun, Mom."

"People will talk. Do you want that? Your coworkers will be whispering behind your back. It can cause irreparable harm to your ability to supervise if they don't respect you."

Sara Beth knew all that, had known it all along without saying the words out loud. "We won't go public with our relationship unless it becomes something more permanent."

"You mean, marriage?" Grace looked shocked, even horrified. She clamped a hand on Sara Beth's arm. "Sweetheart, please don't get your hopes up about such a thing. Ted Bonner is not only a doctor, he's from one of the oldest, wealthiest families in Boston. If you don't think his parents have plans for their only son, you've totally deluded yourself about him."

The bus pulled up, splashing an arc of water onto the sidewalk, making them jump back. Manipulating their umbrellas, they managed a quick, tense hug, then Sara Beth climbed onto the steamy vehicle, the windows too fogged up to see her mother as it pulled away from the curb.

Sara Beth drew a circle on the wet, foggy window, adding two dots for eyes, a short line for a nose, then a down-turned mouth. Her mother was right. Sara Beth *had* gotten her hopes up about Ted, maybe because he was willing to let it be known they were dating, where she'd been cautious because of lifelong warnings from her mother, which had gotten more intense now that Sara Beth was seeing Ted, making it real, not just hypothetical.

Which made Sara Beth also wonder if her mother had experienced what she so fiercely cautioned about. Had she loved a doctor? Been used and dumped? There had to be a reason why she never dated.

As soon as Sara Beth got off the bus, she dialed Ted's number. He picked up right away.

"How was your evening?" he asked.

"I had an incredible *meal*."

He laughed. "See why I don't make a habit of going out to dinner with my parents?"

She smiled. It was obvious that he liked his parents just fine. "How's it going with you? Are you finding anything?"

"It's been interesting. We may have found something. Mostly we think because we're not there anymore, the renewals on the grants probably didn't happen. We don't even know if they replaced us."

"They ran a lousy business," Chance shouted in the background, being much less circumspect than Ted. "Now they're paying for it."

"Except they want us to pay for it, too," Ted added. "At least with our reputation."

Sara Beth dodged a puddle. She picked up speed as the rain started battering her. "What's next?"

"Is it raining?" He went silent for a few seconds. "It's pouring. I hadn't noticed. How close are you to home?"

"I'm running up my walkway right now." She shoved

her key in the lock and rushed inside as a crack of lightning lit up the sky, followed by low, rumbling thunder. "Safe and sound," she said, then climbed the stairs. "So, again, what's next?"

"We're having lunch tomorrow with Ramona, away from the institute. She's doing some research on her own, as well as talking to a lawyer. We ended up telling Paul about the accusations. I didn't want to ask Ramona to keep it from her own fiancé."

"But you're still keeping Derek in the dark?"

"For now."

"I'll let you get back to work, then. My bed's going to be lonely tonight." She smiled at his silence, stuck as he was with Chance within earshot.

"Same here," he said, although not in a sexy way.

She tugged her raincoat off and hung it up outside her front door, toed off her boots, then went inside. "Remember my tiger-striped nightgown?"

"Down to the last detail."

"When you go to bed tonight, picture me wearing that."

"Do you remember the results of that particular experiment?" he asked.

She remembered every erotic detail—the fire in his eyes, the power of his erection, bold and flattering. How he'd looked at her as if she was the only woman in the world. She loved how he could focus like that, and not be distracted.

"I remember," she said, amazed at how aroused she'd become just from the memories. "If you want to call me after Chance leaves and you're in bed, we could talk about it. I've never had phone sex, but it might be an adventure. Not as good as the real thing, of course, but—"

"Experiments are only as effective as the results."

"Then we'll have to test the theory, won't we?" She was caught between pulse-pounding arousal and an image of him being frustrated at not being free to talk, which made her smile.

"It should prove to be an interesting discussion. I'll talk to you later, Sara Beth."

"For sure." She ended the call, shook herself into awareness again, then got ready for bed, keeping her phone close by.

When it rang finally, she drew a settling breath before she answered—to a dial tone. It rang again, then she realized it wasn't her phone but her doorbell. She slid her feet into her teddy-bear slippers and hurried down the stairs.

"Liar," he said, drenched with rain.

He seemed angry. "Ted—"

"I had to park three blocks away, and I ran all the way here, and you're not wearing the tiger. You've got your flannel fire engines on."

She smiled innocently. "It's cold without you."

He picked her up, carried her up the stairs, her pajamas getting wet where they touched him. He went directly into her bedroom, stood her by her bed and un-buttoned her top only enough to yank it over her head.

"I'm not complaining, Sara Beth. I have fond memories of these pajamas." He shoved her bottoms off, kneeling before her, teasing her by trailing his tongue along her skin as he exposed it. Then she helped him get rid of his wet clothes.

"No experiment, after all?" she asked, not at all unhappy about it.

"Did I say that? I think a little experimentation is definitely in order." He backed her up until she came against the bed, then fell onto it. "I think we should see how long it takes to make you beg."

She laughed, breathless and excited. He had her begging almost immediately, but he wouldn't give her the satisfaction of accommodating her, dragging it out until she couldn't think about anything but him, every aspect of him, so that when he finally plunged inside her, she was swept into a climax instantly and held suspended, so that she had no idea how much time passed, five seconds or five minutes. He started to pull out, and she wrapped her legs around him, knew the moment he gave in and let it happen for himself, too. Then he was draped over her, his weight on his arms enough that she could breathe, but his own breathing was heavy, his body adhered to hers.

Awareness crept in, like the sun coming up, first in pink then full light. He lifted his head and met her gaze.

"No protection," they said at the same time.

Then, "I got carried away," also simultaneously, which drew a shaky laugh from her and an even more serious look in his eyes.

"I have never been irresponsible, Sara Beth. I don't know…." He stopped and shook his head, then rolled with her to his side and gathered her close.

"Neither have I." She wanted to ask him what he thought that meant, that two such highly responsible people could be so irresponsible about sex, but she didn't ask, wasn't sure she wanted to know his answer. She only knew how she felt.

She also didn't want to trap him with a pregnancy.

He kissed her hair, tucked her closer, into their usual presleep configuration. "Sleep," he said.

Surprisingly, she did.

Chapter Fourteen

The Coach House Diner was within walking distance of the Armstrong Fertility Institute. Ted and Chance took a late lunch, hoping to avoid the possibility of running into anyone from the institute. Tall, blond Ramona Tate was already seated at a table in the fifties-style diner with its old-fashioned counter and leatherette booths. They hadn't even finished their greetings before Chance was pointing to a booth, tucked back in a corner.

"Let's sit over there. It's a better spot to see who comes in the door," he said. "Have you ordered, Ramona?"

"I was waiting for you."

"Thanks so much for your help," Ted said as they settled into the new booth.

"I get enormous satisfaction catching bad guys in the act."

"Hi, Jenny," Chance said to the waitress who approached with three glasses of ice water. "How are you this beautiful day?"

Because Chance had turned on the famous Demetrios charm, Ted took a closer look at the waitress, who was blond, like Ramona, but curvier.

"Have you looked outside, Dr. Demetrios?" Jenny asked.

"I like the rain. Don't you?"

"I guess that depends on whether I'm already at work or coming to work."

"Makes sense." He ignored the menu she'd set in front of him.

"Your usual?" she asked.

Ted and Ramona exchanged glances. It was as if they didn't exist.

"That'd be great," Chance said, then seemed to wake up to the fact he wasn't alone. "Have you decided?" he asked.

"We haven't had a chance to look at the menu yet." Ted bit back a smile and opened his menu. Ramona did the same, except she was grinning.

"I'll be back in a couple of minutes." Jenny left, without even asking for their drink orders.

"Come here often?" Ted asked Chance, studying the menu.

"Fairly. Why?" The belligerence in his voice made Ted look up.

"What do you recommend?" Ted asked.

Chance settled back, then toyed with his water glass. "I usually get the club sandwich and a cup of vegetable soup."

"Sounds good to me." Ted watched Jenny talk to some customers at the counter while occasionally glancing Chance's way—or maybe she was waiting for Ramona to set aside her menu, too, signaling she'd made her choice.

When their orders were taken and drinks served, they got down to business.

"Paul and I talked about your situation," Ramona said, twirling her engagement ring. "We agree that Breyer is probably being spiteful. If they move ahead with their threat, you'd have legal recourse, but for now, they haven't stated their intentions. So, we need to fight back before it gets to that point. Did you find anything new since we talked last night?"

"We're pretty sure the 'unethical funding' they're referring to is a grant that Breyer accepted from a company called McAdams Fertility Corp. They make a vitamin concoction they bill as a cure. Since we began our own research with a similar base, McAdams had a vested interest in our results."

"Meaning they expected our research to be tilted in their favor," Chance added. "But we didn't go after their money and, in fact, would have rejected the idea of writing a grant for it, had we known. We were forced to accept it, after the fact. That was ultimately what spurred us to move on."

"McAdams probably demanded their money back,"

Ted said. "And Breyer won't refund it, deciding to put the blame on us. We don't know that for sure, but it's the only scenario that makes sense."

"We could also nip this in the bud right now," Chance said with a sideways glance at Ted.

Ted had no doubt what Chance meant. "We're not going down that path. That would make us no better than them."

"Why? What?" Ramona asked.

Chance raised his water glass toward Ted. "We know something they don't think we know."

"And we're not using that knowledge," Ted said. "It doesn't affect patient care, but they *could* lose patients. They may not be cutting-edge in research anymore, but they still do good work with infertility issues."

"Well, if you won't stoop to their level…" Ramona smiled. "Actually, I admire that. It also makes me totally believe you when you say you're innocent. So, let's come up with a plan."

They ate lunch and talked, lingering until Chance was paged to return. He went up to the waitress, Jenny, handed her some money, said something to make her blush, then left.

"Smitten," Ramona said.

"Looks like it."

Ted and Ramona walked back to the institute later, then stood in the hall to finish their conversation.

"So, Ted, were you always this ethical?"

"It's always been important to me," he said, but his thoughts drifted to Sara Beth.

"Do you find it hard to live up to the standards?"

"What? No— Yes." He searched for the right thing to say when his head was filled with the fact he twice hadn't worn a condom with Sara Beth, breaking ethical standards, as Ramona called them. So much for being prepared.

Finally he said, "Doing the right thing matters to me. Always has, always will."

"I hope you're not a dying breed." Ramona opened the door to the employee lounge saying, "I'm going to grab some coffee to take to my office."

Sara Beth almost tumbled out.

Ted caught her before she fell right into Ramona.

"I'm so sorry!" Sara Beth said, straightening. "I'm glad I wasn't carrying a cup of hot coffee."

"Me, too." Ramona smiled. "How are you, Sara Beth?"

Her gaze flickered to Ted briefly then back to Ramona. "I'm very well, thanks. Have you and my favorite quasibrother set a date yet?"

Ramona laughed. "I forget that you and Paul know each other so well. No, not yet. Speaking of siblings, I may have found my half sister."

"Oh, how wonderful! Have you met her?"

"Not yet. We're trying to be sure of the connection. She's apparently an heiress living in New York City. Her name is Victoria Welsh."

"It's good that you're being careful of her feelings. I've heard a lot of stories about children who find out who their donor mother or father is, and have a hard time dealing with it."

"Exactly. We are using caution and care." She touched Ted's arm. "Maybe you don't know what I'm talking about?"

"I'm clueless."

"Sara Beth can fill you in. I don't mind sharing with certain people."

She said goodbye, then Ted and Sara Beth walked to the lab together.

"So, what's her story?" he asked.

"Her mother donated eggs here many years ago, and now she needs a bone-marrow transplant. Ramona isn't a match, so she's been trying to track down possible biological children. Looks like it may happen, after all. It's going to be complicated, no matter how careful they are with this Victoria."

She went quiet, not saying another word until they were inside the lab. They'd started writing the manual that morning, but he'd taken every opportunity to stall. She'd teased him about it.

But the elephant in the room was the fact they'd now slept together twice without protection, and neither of them wanted to talk about it. He guessed he should open the discussion....

"I'm a product of artificial insemination," she said out of the blue.

He just stared at her, at her hands tightly clenched, at how her cheekbones seemed sharp and her face pale.

"I don't know who my father is."

It was the sort of thing Ted wasn't good at—dealing with people's emotional issues, even someone he liked as much as Sara Beth, but he knew he had to say something. "Do you want to know?"

She gave him a sharp look. "Wouldn't you?"

Yes, he probably would. "Your mother won't tell you?"

"The donor was anonymous. My mother had been working here a few years when she decided to do it."

Ted guided Sara Beth to a chair, then sat beside her. "We hear all the time about children who track down donors," he said. "Ramona's a good example. Maybe you could talk to Paul and Lisa about letting you have the information, or letting one of them try to track down the donor, just like Ramona did."

"There's no file. It's gone."

"How do you know?"

"I hunted for it." She hadn't been looking him in the eye. Now she did. "While you were taking up boxes last week."

He wasn't sure what he was feeling about that, except that it didn't sit well. "Why didn't you tell me?"

"Because you're…you. I couldn't involve you." Her smile was small and tight. "And now you know I'm not as ethical as you."

"Under the same circumstances, I'm not sure I wouldn't have done the same thing." He wondered why he wasn't upset by her revelation. In fact, he was more upset that she'd kept it from him until now. No wonder she'd been different last weekend at the shore, less talkative, more distracted. He wished she'd confided in him earlier. That she'd trusted him enough.

"The end justifies the means?" she asked. "That's

generous, but I guess it doesn't matter. My mother said she couldn't leave her own information here for others to see. I understand that. Maybe I'll find it in her personal belongings years from now. Maybe she destroyed it."

Her eyes welled. Ted felt more helpless than he ever had. He rubbed her back. "I can't imagine what that would be like—not knowing."

She pressed the corners of her eyes. "It's gotten harder lately, and I don't even know why. On Valentine's Day—" She stopped, took a shaky breath.

"What happened?" Other than coming to his rescue that day...

"I was in a grocery store, and there was a dad buying a stuffed bear and some candy for his little girl. It about killed me, you know? I never had that, never was daddy's little girl. Sometimes I watch dads playing with kids in the park and my heart hurts. Not just aches, but hurts." She pushed her hand to her mouth. "I'm sorry for dumping this on you. I was excited for Ramona to find that connection—not only to help her mother, but because it also gives her a sister. It just hit me hard. I'll be fine. Really."

She got up. "I'll be back."

Ted didn't move for a minute, then he opened a desk drawer and took out an employee roster. It hadn't been updated since Sara Beth's mother had retired. He found Grace O'Connell's address, wrote it down, stuffed it in his pocket.

After all that Sara Beth had done for him, it was time he returned the favor.

And what if she *was* pregnant? He needed to step up to the plate *now*.

He left her a note, then for the first time in his life, played hooky from work.

He should have called first—etiquette demanded it—but he was afraid she wouldn't agree to see him. So, he surprised Grace O'Connell, ambushed her by showing up on her doorstep.

He hesitated when he saw her, because either she suffered from allergies or she'd been crying. Should he ask what was wrong? She probably wouldn't answer. Why would she, without knowing him? He was grateful, at least, that they'd met in the lobby at the institute, so she recognized him.

"This isn't a good time," she said.

"I wouldn't bother you if it wasn't extremely important, Ms. O'Connell. Please. Just a few minutes of your time."

"All right," she said with obvious reluctance.

Ted stepped inside, noticing that she and her daughter had similar styles in furnishings and art.

"Thank you for seeing me."

"You didn't give me a lot of choice, did you? Have a seat."

He saw Sara Beth in her, different hair and eye color, but similarities in their facial structure and body type.

She sat in a chair across from him. "What can I do for you?"

"I've been seeing your daughter."

"She told me."

Okay. That made it easier. He didn't have to break that particular ice. "Sara Beth talked with me today about how she was conceived."

Her mouth hardened. "I see."

"It weighs on her a lot that she doesn't know who fathered her."

"You're not telling me something I haven't known for most of her life." Her fingers curved into the chair arms. "Your point is?"

"She's in a great deal of pain because of it. I don't like to see her in pain."

"Do you think I do? You think it gives me pleasure to see her struggle with it?" Her voice kept rising as she defended herself. "What kind of mother do you think I am?"

"A loving one, according to Sara Beth. Except with regard to this particular issue, I gather."

She calmed a little. "My hands are tied by anonymity. You know how that works, right, *Dr.* Bonner?"

"Please call me Ted. Of course I do. Which is why I'm offering to track down the father and see if he's interested in meeting her—without involving her in the search, or getting her hopes up."

"My daughter suggested that very thing last night. So, you're the intermediary she chose?"

"We didn't discuss it. And she has no idea I've come to see you. It's just something I'd like to do for her."

"Why?"

"Why not? She means a lot to me." *She might be the mother of my child.*

She smiled tightly. "And you think this would make her happy?"

Ted didn't know what to make of the woman whom Sara Beth sang the praises of. He was finding her aloof and not very maternal. Why wouldn't she want Sara Beth to be happy?

"I know she's unhappy not knowing," Ted said.

"There's no guarantee that would change if she got the information she thinks she wants."

"True. But the curiosity she's lived with would be satisfied. She could move forward, one way or the other. She's long been an adult. It's time to stop treating her like a child."

It was the wrong thing to say. He saw that right away. Her expression closed up tight.

"She *is* a child, Dr. Bonner. *My* child. That will never change. And until you have a child of your own, you won't understand how strong that bond is, especially the need to protect your child from hurt. You think it will help her to find who fathered her? I don't."

"She's your daughter, Ms. O'Connell, and always will be. But she's no longer your child."

Grace stood. "It's time for you to go."

He'd already risen automatically because she had. Now he went to the door, guilt settling on his shoulders. He'd meant to help Sara Beth. Instead, he may have hurt her cause even more. "Thank you for your time."

"You haven't asked me not to tell Sara Beth about this," she said as he stepped outside.

"You won't have to. I plan to tell her myself."

"Ah. Honesty is the best policy?"

He smiled, more at himself than her, then recited his mantra. "I was an Eagle Scout."

"I guess that explains a lot," Grace said. "Maybe I should be just as direct with you."

"Please do."

"My daughter generally puts other people's needs before her own. It's part of what makes her a good nurse. But she's also gotten hurt because of it."

He considered that. *Don't mess with my daughter,* was what she meant. It was true that Sara Beth had often put his needs first. He'd been trying to pay her back some today, but without success.

"I hear you," Ted said. "Thank you for giving me a chance to speak. I hope you change your mind, sooner rather than later."

"Well, that day may, indeed, come. Who knows?"

He didn't know how to take that, but ultimately, it didn't matter.

The only thing that mattered now was how Sara Beth felt about what he'd done.

Sara Beth kept herself busy in the clinical wing. Ted had disappeared right after she'd shared her secret with him. He'd seemed okay with what she'd told him, but then he'd left the clinic for parts unknown, only leaving behind a note saying he'd let her know when he got back.

Chance's consultation room door opened and a couple came out, the Lombards, both of them smiling, the woman crying. Sara Beth recognized happy tears when she saw them.

"Did you hear, Sara Beth?" Mary Lombard said. "Twins. We're having twins. It's a miracle."

Sara Beth hugged her. "That is the best possible news. Congratulations to both of you."

They floated away, as delighted, expectant couples tended to do, one of the things that made her work fulfilling. She never tired of offering her congratulations, never tired of seeing their ecstatic faces when their children came into the world.

Sara Beth's pager went off. She figured Chance wanted her or Ted had returned, but it was Wilma Goodheart, asking her to come to reception. Sara Beth's footsteps slowed as she spotted Tricia Trahearn in the lobby, studying one of the paintings.

"I told her Dr. Bonner was out of the building, so she asked for you," Wilma said.

"Thank you, Ms. Goodheart." Sara Beth approached Tricia, who was wearing an expensive-looking black suit, probably Armani or some other designer.

"Hello, Tricia," Sara Beth said when she got within earshot. She thought she remembered the woman accurately, how voluptuous she was, as evidenced by her red dress on Valentine's Day, but this time she looked professional, more…judgelike.

"Hello, Sara Beth." She extended her hand. "My vacation has come to an end, and I'm heading home to Vermont. I wanted to say goodbye to Ted, but I understand he's not here."

"He'll be back, although I don't know when. It's already close to quitting time, so you probably wouldn't have long to wait. Do you want to do that or is there a message I can give him?"

She glanced at her watch. "I need to get on the road. If you would please tell him I enjoyed seeing him again, and that I hope we can stay in touch."

"I'll be happy to."

Tricia leaned close. "We went out to dinner once, but there was nothing else to it."

Sara Beth smiled. "He told me."

Tricia smiled back. "I reminded Ted that night and I'll caution you. His parents' expectations are high. They were friendly to you at dinner because their manners are impeccable, but if they thought for a minute that things were really serious between you and Ted? Who knows?"

"Why are you telling me?"

"For Ted's sake. Because I think you need to decide how important your relationship is. If you end up making him choose between you and his parents, and you're not serious about him, it might take a while for the rift to heal. In case you haven't figured it out already, Ted doesn't make waves. Doesn't like waves."

Yes, Sara Beth had noticed that. He avoided conflict, but so did she. Which was probably why they hadn't discussed the possibility she could be pregnant. They should. "I appreciate your directness," Sara Beth said.

The subject of their conversation paged her then, saying he was back. He'd probably come in the employee's entrance.

"He's returned," she said after barely a moment's hesitation. "I'll take you to him."

"Never mind. Just tell him goodbye, please. It's good enough."

On her way to the lab, Sara Beth stopped by the clinic to see if she was needed for anything, then continued on, hoping she was going to learn why Ted had disappeared.

"You're back," she said as she went inside the lab. "Just in time to go home."

"I'm going to work late tonight to make up for it."

"Of course you are." She smiled. "I can stay, too, if you want to work on the manual."

He put on his lab coat. "I have some other things to do."

He wasn't being cool, exactly, but he wasn't making eye contact, either.

"Tricia was just here. She's headed back to Vermont and wanted to say goodbye."

He nodded. She waited, wondering if he would say where he'd gone, but he turned on his computer and stared at the screen.

"I'll see you later, then," she said, wondering if she would, Tricia's caution still echoing in her head.

"Sara Beth."

"Yes?"

"I went to see your mother."

She took a couple of steps toward him. "Why?"

"To try to convince her to find out who your father is." He finally looked at her. "I wasn't successful in doing anything but irritating her."

She nodded, unable to speak.

"She wasn't happy to see me, although it also seemed she was upset about something before I got there." He took her hand. "I'm sorry."

"I appreciate that you tried."

"Do you? I know I should've asked you first, but my plan was to get the information then pass it along only if I was successful. I didn't want to get your hopes up."

She squeezed his hand, wishing she could just throw herself into his arms. Then suddenly she found she could smile. He'd done a wonderful thing, trying to help her. She appreciated that. Him.

"Thank you so much," she said.

"It's the thought that counts?"

"There was action involved, too. Will you come to my place after you're done here?"

"I'll even bring dinner."

"That's a deal." She went toward the door then turned around. "I like you a whole lot." It was the closest she could come to telling him she loved him, something she knew he wasn't ready to hear now, if ever.

He grinned. "Ditto."

The fact he'd remembered her saying that to him before kept her smiling—until nine o'clock came and he hadn't shown up or answered his cell phone.

She finally gave up at eleven-fifteen and went to bed, was almost asleep when her doorbell rang. She trudged downstairs and let him in, the cold air waking her up more than she wanted to be.

"Are you hungry?" she asked.

"Yeah. For you." He hauled her to him and kissed her, long and thoroughly. "I'm sorry I didn't call. I got lost in the work."

"It's fine. Truly it is." She cupped his face. "I admire your dedication, Ted. But…" She went up on tiptoe to kiss him.

"But?"

"Tomorrow I'm giving you your own key."

He went silent. "Are you sure?" he asked finally.

She nodded. She'd never been surer. "I don't want to go downstairs in the cold to let you in."

That was the least of it, and they both knew it. Giving him a key was a commitment.

"Okay?" she asked, holding her breath.

"Okay." Then he slipped his arm around her waist and walked upstairs with her, where he warmed her up in a hurry—and never mentioned giving her a key to his loft in return.

Chapter Fifteen

The following Monday morning, Sara Beth was working with Ted and Chance. The research protocols for the best-practices manual were complete. They'd started on the clinical protocols, which would take a few days more. They didn't have to work in the lab, but by unspoken agreement were doing just that.

A knock came on the door window. Ramona stood there, framed by the glass, smiling.

"She looks too happy," Chance said, letting her in.

"I would've brought champagne," Ramona said, "but I knew I couldn't bring it in here. Oh, how cute," she said, distracted momentarily as she picked up two small stuffed bears, one pink and one blue, from Sara Beth's desk.

"For the Johnson twins, born yesterday," Sara Beth

said as Ramona gave them back. She hugged them, loving the feel of their silky soft fur, the bears her traditional gift for every new baby at the clinic. She kept a scrapbook of photographs of the parents, babies and bears when the babies were dressed in their going-home outfits.

"Well, the Johnsons are celebrating and so can you," Ramona said to Ted and Chance. "You have been vindicated."

The sound that came from both men blended laughter and relief.

"How'd you manage that so fast?" Ted asked.

"Thanks to your meticulous records, which proved you didn't apply for the McAdams grant, *and* copies of your e-mails expressing your desire not to accept the grant, *plus* a pithily stated letter from the institute's attorney—" she stopped and drew a breath "—their claim has been declared null and void."

"Did you get it in writing?" Chance asked.

She passed them each a sheet of paper. "I don't think you'll hear from them again. Now, get back to the work you're supposed to be doing." She left, a bounce in her step.

Sara Beth whooped with joy. Ted and Chance grinned ear to ear, punching each other's shoulders. She knew how much the unjust claim had weighed on them.

"Let's try to avoid any more scandals, Chance," Ted said.

"You're directing that at me? I've been behaving myself. Have you?"

Sara Beth's cell phone rang before he could answer.

She saw it was her mother and handed the bears to Ted, laughing as he dangled them by the scuffs of their necks in front of him.

"Hi, Mom!"

A beat passed. "You sound chipper."

"That's a good word for it. What's up?"

"I need to talk to you."

"Oh. Okay. Hold on. I'll find an empty office—"

"Not on the phone. Please, Sara Beth. I need you to come here to the house. Right now."

"You want me to leave work?"

"Yes."

Since her mother was the original never-miss-a-day workaholic, Sara Beth knew it must be serious. "All right. I'll be there as soon as possible."

"Something wrong?" Ted asked as she took the bears from him and got her purse from the drawer.

"I don't know. My mom issued a command performance. I have to go." She could tell he wanted to ask more questions, but couldn't in front of Chance. "I'll be back as soon as I can."

Sara Beth fretted all the way to her mother's house. The only other time she could remember her mother sounding so upset was when *her* mother had died ten years ago. That mother-daughter relationship had been tense and tentative for as long as Sara Beth could remember, yet her mother had mourned deeply. Maybe because it hadn't been a good relationship? Sara Beth had wondered. Her mother told her once that she'd made a conscious decision to be a better mother than her own, a more loving one.

And except for the one big issue between them, Sara Beth agreed that her mother had succeeded. Their relationship was closer than most of her friends had with their mothers, although Sara Beth didn't want to disappoint her mother by having gotten pregnant. She wished she knew if she was.

Sara Beth jogged from the bus stop to her mother's house and went inside. Grace stood at the front window, her arms folded across her stomach, her face ashen.

"What's wrong?" Sara Beth rushed to her mother's side.

"I didn't want to tell you, sweetheart. Not ever. Now I'm being forced to. I'm sorry. I'm so sorry."

Sara Beth took her mother by the hand and led her to the sofa, sitting right next to her.

"This is how the rich and powerful operate, Sara Beth. I've told you for years. Now you'll know."

"Know what, Mom?"

"Emily Armstrong is gunning for your termination at the institute."

Sara Beth's first thought was that her and Ted's…relationship had been discovered. But the institute didn't have a nonfraternization rule, so what difference would that make? "Why?"

Grace put her face in her hands for a moment, her legs bouncing, then she looked her daughter in the eye. "Because she found out I spent two weeks with Gerald. He called me last week—the day Ted came to see me, in fact. Gerald warned me then that Emily knew. I've been waiting to see what would happen. Today I found out."

"Wait. Go back. Are you saying you went away with Dr. Armstrong? When?"

"When I said I was in Cancún. Emily went to Greece on vacation. She put Gerald in a private spa while she was gone to see if physical therapy could help him."

"Did it?"

"Not much. He's still using a wheelchair most of the time. I helped oversee his care, so I saw for myself how bad off he is. I hadn't seen him since he retired."

"I don't understand. Did you go there as his nurse?"

"I went as his friend. His longtime, caring friend. But Emily had forbidden contact between us outside of the institute, which I had respected—until Gerald called and asked if I'd join him."

"I've always known that Mrs. Armstrong didn't like you—and me, for years now—but to forbid contact? Why? Why is she so worried about your friendship with Dr. Armstrong? And what does it have to do with me?"

"Oh, sweetheart. Gerald Armstrong is your father."

The words landed hard on Sara Beth, a gut punch that drove her backward. "You…used—Mom, you used *his* sperm?"

Grace didn't answer, just looked at Sara Beth as if she could read her mother's mind. Then she did. Clearly. Vividly. Everything made sense now. Everything.

"You had an affair with him."

"Yes."

"You got pregnant with me."

"Yes."

Nausea, hot and sickening, rose in Sara Beth. She'd

thought she wanted to know. Thought it would complete her life. But not this. Not this.

She stood, her knees wobbling, and made her way to the front window, seeing nothing, feeling the pain of her mother's deception. "That means...Lisa is my sister. And Olivia."

"Yes."

She had brothers, too—Paul and Derek. "Lisa was born only a month after me."

Grace came up beside her. "Gerald and Emily had reconciled some major differences. We told everyone I'd gone through artificial insemination. Even Emily believed it. Then you were born, and as you got older, it was apparent you were an Armstrong."

"There is a painting on the staircase of Dr. Armstrong's mother." Sara Beth pressed the heels of her hands to her eyes, recalling a dim memory of the portrait. "Paul and Derek used to tease me about being a long, lost Armstrong. I looked so much like their grandmother.

"Emily confronted Gerald," Grace said. "He admitted to it."

"It was when I was fourteen. Wasn't it? Everything changed then."

"Yes."

"How long did your—" she could barely say the word "—affair last?"

"As I said, they'd been having marital problems. I had fallen in love with him years before, but had never acted on it, never said a word. Then he needed me, and

I gave in to my feelings. We were together for about a month, then he went back to her, and we never slept together again. We hugged each other once, just once. Right after you were born."

"He never came to see me?"

"He saw you, but at his house. Emily offered to keep you during the day, to share their nanny. You remember that, I'm sure. It saved me a lot of money, but, selfishly, I wanted you to know your siblings."

"Didn't he give you financial support?"

"He helped me to buy this house, but no monthly support, at my request. Then he made sure I was well taken care of in retirement. It was his way of assuring you an inheritance, through me."

Not ready to deal with it yet, Sara Beth ignored the revelation that Dr. Armstrong was her father. "How could you stand it, Mom? How could you work with him every day, side by side, loving him, not being with him? Why didn't you get a job somewhere else?"

"You say you're in love with Ted Bonner. If you are, you can answer that question yourself."

She shook her head. She could not do that, could not wait for a man to love her back, to be free to love her publicly.

"I have never admired or respected any man as I did Gerald, sweetheart."

"You denied me a father, even a stepfather, because you couldn't give up a fantasy, Mom. A fantasy!" She gestured wildly. "I thought you had your act together better than any woman I know. I've always admired you. Now I don't know what to think. What to believe. And that I could lose the job I love, too? What am I supposed to do about that?"

"I think we need to call Emily's bluff. She says she'll tell everyone that you're Gerald's daughter, making it too difficult for you to continue working there. She knows you're not only tenderhearted, but that you would never hurt Lisa."

"Why would she expose her husband's infidelity like that? Does she hate him so much?"

"I think she hates me more and therefore, you. But I truly believe she's bluffing. She's grasping at straws out of anger that I was with him for those two weeks, sharing his confidences."

"I don't blame her."

Grace assumed a defensive stance. "This is the first time it's happened. And obviously it wasn't physical."

"Mom, put yourself in her shoes. She must have forgiven him or at least accepted that your affair ended, even though I was a visible reminder ever since. But I don't think it's the physical infidelity she resents anymore. It's the emotional one. Two weeks with a former lover? The mother of your child? That would be hard for anyone to swallow."

Grace burst into tears. "I know, Sara Beth. I know. I'm so angry at myself. My instinct was to say no when Gerald asked me to come. I should've listened to my instincts. I should've respected Emily."

Sara Beth offered no comfort, wasn't ready to hug her mother as if nothing had happened.

"I'm glad you see that, Mom." But Sara Beth could see her own truth, too. That except for the fact that Ted wasn't married, Sara Beth could be in the same position as her mother had been, single and pregnant. She couldn't lose her job, too.

"I have to talk to her. Mrs. Armstrong. I have to get her to see that I won't tell anyone, that I'll take the secret to my grave."

"She won't see you."

"I have to try. And I have to see Dr. Armstrong, knowing he's my father, and that's he's known all this time and kept it to himself. I have to be able to understand how he could do that."

Sara Beth needed to think back through the years and try to remember any time he'd treated her daughterlike. She needed to get away from the one person she'd trusted most in her life, the one she'd never thought would break that trust, and yet who had lied to her all her life.

"*She* especially won't let you see him," Grace said, insistent. "He stays in bed. He wouldn't even know you were there, trying to see him. There's no way around it."

"If he knew that I knew the truth, would he? Would he talk to me?"

"If Emily weren't around? Yes, I think he would. He regrets keeping it—you—a secret. You know that Emily and Ted's mother are friends, right?"

The sudden shift in subject made Sara Beth frown. "Acquaintances, I think. Same-social-circle kind of thing."

"Which means that Emily has influence there, too. It would only take a sly comment."

Sara Beth clenched her fists, anger coiled inside her with no way to release it. She had to leave. That was the only thing she knew for sure.

"You know, Mom, it was only a couple of weeks ago that you said if I couldn't be public about a relationship, something wasn't right about it."

"And that was experience talking. Do what I say, you know, not what I do."

Sara Beth nodded, wishing that could be enough of an answer. She didn't want to talk anymore. "Give me some time, Mom. I'll be in touch when I can think more clearly."

"I love you, baby." Despair layered her barely uttered words.

"I know." Sara Beth closed her eyes against the pain. "I love you, too. I just don't like you very much right now."

She hurried out the front door. Where to go? What to do?

Ted kept an eye on the lab door, accomplishing so little he might as well just stop working altogether. He'd never experienced anything like it before.

Where was she? Why hadn't she returned? Why hadn't she at least called?

He'd never worried about someone like this. For her mother to demand her to leave work, it must be something huge. Sara Beth would need him....

Ted shoved his hands through his hair, much shorter now that he'd finally gotten a haircut. He stared at the employee parking lot, although he knew she would return by bus, and come in the front entrance.

He wandered away, tempted to go to the lobby and wait, tempted to call her, but resisting. He didn't want to add to the problem, whatever it was.

His gaze landed on the pink and blue teddy bears, which reminded him of her pain over not knowing a father, that special relationship between father and daughter.

A reminder, too, that she could be pregnant.

They hadn't talked about it. She hadn't brought it up, and he'd been wrapped up in worry about getting his name cleared. Now that was done. For good, he hoped.

The door swung open. Sara Beth came in, looking much like her mother had when he'd gone to see her, although more hollow-eyed than teary. She made an effort to smile.

He went toward her, needed to grab her tight and hold on, for his sake as much as hers. "Are you all right?"

She put out a hand, preventing him from getting closer. "I came to get the bears. It's my only chance to take the Johnsons' picture. They're on their way home to Quincy." She sidestepped around him, picked up the bears, clutched them.

She looked…lost. He wanted her to confide in him, to break down in his arms if that was what she needed. He wanted to be the only man with the right to do that.

He wanted to make babies with her. Maybe he already had. And he didn't want any child of his to grow up without both parents in a loving home.

"Marry me," he said.

She jerked back. Her expression was one either of shock or horror. "What?"

"Marry me. Please."

"Ted, please. I can't deal with this right now. Everything is too raw."

"Raw? In what way? You can't deal with a marriage proposal?"

"Not right now. I have to go. Please leave me alone for now. I have a lot to think about." She rushed out, leaving him standing and staring and bewildered.

Chance came in before the door had closed all the way. "What's going on with Sara Beth? It's like she didn't even see me."

"She's upset about something."

"That call from her mother?"

"I would assume, yes."

Chance laid a hand on Ted's shoulder. "And what's your excuse? You look like hell."

He spoke without thinking. "I proposed to her. She didn't seem to appreciate it." An understatement, he thought.

"Proposed? I didn't know you were dating."

"For a month or so. She could be pregnant, Chance."

Chance dropped into a chair. "You're the last person I ever would've thought might accidentally get a woman pregnant."

"I'm a little stunned myself." He sat down next to his friend. "I don't want anyone to think we had to get married. I want her to marry me so there's no question about it."

"So you want to marry her whether or not she's pregnant?"

"Yeah." It struck him like lightning then. He loved her. Forever-after loved her.

"So," Chance drawled. "Knowing you as I do, I'm going to guess that you proposed without the trappings."

"Trappings? I don't know what you mean."

"The traditional big deal, Ted. The roses and candlelight and perfect meal. The pledge of undying love. The special moment she'll want to paste in her mental scrapbook forever. Those trappings. The bare essentials."

He hadn't even come close. He hadn't even told her that he loved her. They'd been standing in the research lab. He should have told her. "I screwed it up. Big-time. No wonder she didn't appreciate it." Well, that and whatever her mother had said to her. His lack of sensitivity wasn't anything new, he supposed, but she was different. He'd noticed she was upset, but hadn't taken it into consideration, just forged ahead with his proposal as if her feelings hadn't mattered. He wasn't usually so egotistical.

"It's not too late," Chance said. "It'll just take some planning. If you're interested, I've got some ideas."

They came up with a plan, which was good, because Ted liked plans he could follow. Then he made phone calls to set the works in motion.

He was planning more than the bare essentials, but would it be enough?

Chapter Sixteen

The beautiful house where Sara Beth had spent a good deal of her childhood seemed cold now, and unwelcoming. She climbed the steps and rang the bell, her heart heavy, her legs feeling like she wore concrete shoes.

The door opened. Sara Beth thought she might get sick right there on the landing.

"What are you doing here?" Emily Armstrong asked, her tone haughtier than usual.

"I need to talk to you. Please."

"We have nothing to say." She started to shut the door.

"Don't make me create a scene. I will try, if I have to, to be loud enough that…Dr. Armstrong could hear me."

"Blackmail? How lovely." But she allowed Sara Beth

inside, took her to the dayroom that was Emily's personal space, a sunny, feminine room. "Make it fast."

Sara Beth hadn't been invited to sit, so she didn't. "My mother told me everything this morning."

"I thought she would." Emily took a seat in a flower-upholstered wingback chair that looked like a throne.

"I only want one thing, Mrs. Armstrong. A chance to talk to Dr.—my father. Just once. Then I'll leave you both alone. And in return you have my promise to keep the secret forever."

"And quit your job."

"I can't do that."

"Then, no deal."

"What do you expect to gain by telling everyone about me? About your husband's affair? How is that better than me simply keeping the secret?"

Her eyes turned icy. "He broke his promise to me. He said he would never see her alone again."

"So, it's revenge? What will it gain you?"

"Sympathy, I imagine."

"I understand he broke your trust. I would be furious and hurt, too. But telling the world will only hurt your children."

She picked a piece of lint off her sharply creased pants. "The casualties of war."

Sara Beth decided her mother was right. Emily was bluffing. She would not hurt her children that way.

"Until I was fourteen," Sara Beth said, "I loved you like a second mother. I thought you were so elegant, such a lady. And I always appreciated how you let me hang out here, and let Lisa spend the night with me, how you accepted me as part of your family. When that changed—when I was fourteen and you found out about me, I guess—I was devastated. I didn't know what I'd done. I cried about it a lot. Lisa's and my relationship faltered until we both started college, and she didn't have to account for her whereabouts anymore."

Sara Beth approached Emily, understanding how hurt she'd been that her husband had strayed—and with a woman whose child she'd accepted almost as her own, not knowing the connection. "Thank you for what you gave me. I appreciate it more than I can say. But I'm not leaving the institute. It's my home and my passion."

She walked out of the room, hoping Emily would follow her, to say it would be all right for her to see her father.

It didn't happen. She wasn't hailed back. And when she got home, there was no message on her answering machine saying she'd changed her mind, and to please return.

The silence was devastating.

Now what? It wasn't worth going back to work for the short time that remained of the workday, to try to pretend that her world hadn't just been turned upside down. She didn't want to see Ted, either—

Ted. He'd asked her to marry him.

Where had that come from? *Marry me,* he'd said. That was all.

She wasn't pregnant—well, she didn't know if she was pregnant—so why had he bothered? If he'd loved her, he would've said so. And then there was the issue with his parents, who had plans for their son. Plans that didn't include a woman who couldn't admit that the famous family tree she'd come from had to be kept secret—and who was also the result of an affair, anyway.

Not exactly parent-pleasing credentials.

She wanted to cry, to throw things, to stomp and wail and rend clothing. Instead she crawled into bed and pulled the quilt over her head. It didn't stop the thoughts from swirling. She needed to get out of the house, focus on something else for a while—

As if she could really be distracted. Right. Sure.

Sara Beth flopped the bedding away from her face, ready to take some kind of action. Ted loomed over her.

She gasped, her heart pounding. She couldn't scrape out a word.

"I want to take you someplace," he said quietly, gently, sitting beside her.

"Okay."

A beat passed. "That was easier than I expected."

He hadn't known her thoughts. He'd just come along at the right time, a lifeguard tossing a float to a drowning victim.

He held out a hand to her, helping her stand up. She saw him look her over, and take note that she was still wearing her shoes while in bed.

"Want to talk about it?" he asked.

"Not yet." Maybe not ever. She didn't know if she would ever tell another living soul what she'd learned today. "You proposed to me," she said, deciding to jump that hurdle before it blocked their way.

He smiled a little. "Let's just shelve that for now, okay? Let's just go have some fun."

Startled, worried that they *would* have to talk about it, she agreed instantly. "That's a deal."

She finally noticed he was wearing a suit—and a crisp white shirt and red tie. Red? It was so un-Ted-like, she ran her hand down it, then patted his stomach. He sucked it in.

"Where are we going?" she asked.

"It's a surprise."

She studied his face and the tender expression that she didn't dare try to interpret. "I'm guessing I should dress up?"

"That dress you wore on my birthday brings back fond memories, especially what you wore underneath."

"You mean my fabulous muscle tone?" The fact she could joke said a lot about how comfortable she felt with him. His expression changed, too, from concerned to relieved.

He slid his arms around her waist, moved his hands down her rear, bringing her hips to his. "Anytime you need to talk, I'm here, Sara Beth."

"I know that. For tonight, this girl just wants to have fun."

He kissed her before he let her go, the softest, most tender kiss he'd ever given her. Tears pricked her eyes. She hugged him hard, then she went to make herself look beautiful, figuring that at some point he would either repeat the proposal or apologize for it.

She wasn't sure which she wanted to hear, was ready to hear. It was all too much at once....

Which was a lie. She wanted him to repeat it.

"First a limo and now a private jet?" Sara Beth stared out the car window at the sleek jet with the stairs leading up to it. "How did you swing this? And why?"

"I wanted to wine and dine you in style. Something wrong with that? The plane belongs to an old friend, Rourke Devlin. A fellow Eagle Scout, by the way. It's how we met."

"I like him already." She smiled, took one last bite of a strawberry, then finished the sparkling cider in her flute. She hadn't commented on the lack of champagne, knowing he was just looking out for her in case she was pregnant, which meant he was as aware of the possibility as she was. She'd accepted the glass without a word.

The limo driver opened the door and helped her out. Ted followed, took her hand and led her up the stairs into the plane. "This is so much fun!" she said. "Thank you."

"The night has just begun."

She wouldn't have guessed he had a lot of romantic gestures in his arsenal, and maybe she was being hit by every one of them tonight, but it didn't matter if it was a one-time adventure. She wanted the memory.

Tomorrow she would have to face her future—whatever Emily Armstrong decided to do—but tonight she would enjoy herself.

"So are you going to tell me where we're going?" she asked, when she was buckled in.

"New York City." He presented her with another glass of sparkling cider and a tray of appetizers—prosciutto-wrapped asparagus, a variety of cheese and crackers, more strawberries. "To tide you over."

There was so much to talk about, yet neither of them did much talking. They looked out the window, tried to identify cities and landmarks, kept things light and simple, while beneath the surface, emotions bubbled, at least for her.

She caught him staring at her, his expression so serious that she cupped his face and kissed him before he said anything to change the happy mood.

Another limo awaited them. They were whisked away to Central Park, where a carriage took them for a long spin around the park, the night cold and clear. She couldn't remember them ever saying so little. Until now, they'd always had things to say.

By the time they reached the famous Boat House restaurant, tension had wrapped around them. They were seated at a table overlooking the lake.

She didn't think she could eat a thing, she'd gotten so worked up. Whatever had made her think she could just have an evening of fun with him? She'd learned today that her mother had had an affair with a man Sara Beth had known all her life, without knowing he was her father. That his wife was justifiably angry about it, but planning to take revenge on Sara Beth, the innocent victim in the whole affair.

And the man she loved had parents who would never accept her. Yet if she was pregnant, she wanted to marry him....

She wanted to marry him anyway, but she didn't want to burden him with the fact she was not just a child of artificial insemination, lacking the knowledge of her father's identity, but instead the child of an illicit affair, her father a wealthy, powerful man to rival Ted's own.

"You've stopped having fun," Ted said, after the waiter had taken their order for Caesar salad and grilled swordfish.

"I'm sorry to ruin the beautiful evening you planned. It's wonderful, truly. I'm just..." Her burdens came crashing down. She couldn't keep them at bay for much longer. She was ready to fall apart, ready to cry.

She'd put off reacting to everything she'd learned—had it just been today? Now she had to pay the consequences.

Ted gave her a long look then signaled the waiter and whispered something to him. He returned in a moment with a silver covered dish and presented it to Sara Beth, pulling off the lid, revealing a nosegay of white roses.

Ted reached for her hand. "I love you, Sara Beth."

She pressed her face into the fragrant bouquet, her eyes stinging, her throat burning, heart racing. When she lifted her head, Ted was beside her, on one knee, holding an open ring box with a gorgeous diamond and sapphire engagement ring.

"I love you. I want to spend my days and nights with you. Please marry me."

She looked into his hopeful eyes and saw true love there. More than anything she wanted to say yes, but what came out was, "I can't."

Chapter Seventeen

Stunned, Ted watched Sara Beth run off. Everyone was staring at the man on bended knee, the meaning of which couldn't have been lost on anyone. In that scenario, however, usually the woman smiled, misted up, said an enthusiastic yes and threw her arms around the man.

Chance had been wrong. Even the trappings hadn't mattered. She didn't love him—yet—in return. He should've waited for her to say it first. Now he'd embarrassed them both.

Ted canceled their dinner order, since he was sure she wouldn't want to sit there and have dinner as if nothing had happened. He dropped the ring box in his pocket. She'd taken the bouquet with her.

"Sir?" The waiter leaned close to him. "We think your companion needs you."

Ted sprang up. "Where is she?"

"The ladies' room, sir." He pointed. "Through there and to the right."

Ladies' room? How was he supposed to help her there? "Did she ask for me?"

"No, sir, but she is apparently having some difficulty—"

Ted took off running. He didn't hesitate when he got to the restroom but slammed the door open and rushed in. He found her on a small sofa, crying like he'd never seen anyone cry before. It broke his heart.

"Sara Beth," he said softly, soothingly.

She went silent for a moment. "Go away." She started crying again, trying so hard not to that her whole body shook.

"I'm not going away." He looked around for some tissue, found a box and passed her a few, then he sat beside her.

The door opened. A woman looked inside, saw them, then backed out.

"You're in the ladies' room," Sara Beth told him, wiping her eyes.

"There's a first time for everything."

"Dr. Armstrong is my father."

He almost didn't catch what she said. She had the tissues pressed to her nose and wasn't looking at him. After a moment the words sank in.

"Is that what your mother told you today?"

She nodded. "I said I wouldn't tell anyone, but you're a doctor. You have to keep secrets."

He didn't remind her that she wasn't his patient and this wasn't a medical issue, because it didn't make any difference. He would never share her secret.

"So, Dr. Armstrong was using his own sperm to help impregnate the women who came to the clinic?" he said. "That's happened before, unfortunately."

"No, Ted. They had an affair," she whispered.

Ted felt his jaw drop. Because she started to cry again, he wrapped his arms around her and didn't let go as she told him the whole story, including how she'd gone to see Emily Armstrong.

After a while, a knock came on the door, and the manager came in, saying that if they needed a private place, he could let them use his office.

They decided to return to where the limo waited for them. She clutched the bouquet, but barely made eye contact with Ted.

The driver took them to a building on Park Avenue.

"Where are we?" she asked.

"Rourke's penthouse. He's out of town. In Boston, actually. He said we were welcome to use it tonight…." Of course, Ted had thought they would be celebrating.

"I didn't bring anything with me to stay over."

He'd had fun buying something red and lacy, but now didn't seem to be the time to bring it up. "It doesn't matter. You must be tired."

She nodded, although her spirits seemed to be on

the mend. He took advantage of the moment, in case he was right.

"One question first, please, then I won't bring it up again." Tonight, anyway. He wrapped her hands in his. "Do you love me?"

She didn't say anything for a few seconds, then finally, as if she was in pain, "Yes. With all my heart."

Relief struck first, then he dug for patience, usually easy to find. "Then why can't you marry me?"

"If I'm pregnant, we'll talk about it again. Maybe I should take a test. It might give us an answer."

"I don't want to know. I don't care. It doesn't make a difference to me if you're pregnant or not. I want to marry you, no matter what. Right now."

She swallowed. He thought he'd finally gotten through to her, until she said, "Have you thought about your parents?"

"What? What about them?"

"They have big plans for you. They want you to marry a woman of your own kind."

He almost laughed. "My own kind?"

"You know what I mean. Not the daughter of—" She shook her head. "I'm so used to not knowing half of my parentage. Now, instead of thinking I was conceived scientifically, I have to remember I was conceived when my father cheated on his wife. What do you think your parents will think of that?"

"It's none of their business. That's what I think."

"Well, *I* think they love you and want you to marry the right person."

Her logic, or lack thereof, was starting to make its own kind of sense. "So, let me get this straight. You love me, but you won't marry me, even though I don't care whether you're pregnant or not, because you think my parents might disown me or something?" He waited for her to confirm it. When she didn't, he cupped her face, making her look into his eyes, willing her to see what was in his heart. "Marry me. Tonight. We'll take Rourke's jet and fly to Las Vegas. I want to have the right to show that I love you in public. And if you happen to be pregnant already, I'd rather no one know we jumped the gun. Not for me, Sara Beth, but for you, and our child, if there is one. Let me protect you from the gossip, please. Marry me tonight."

"Okay." Her voice was breathless and full of joy. "I love you, Ted."

He grinned and finally kissed her, said he loved her again, then dug into his pocket for the ring. He slipped it on her finger, pressed his lips to the soft skin above it, then tucked both of her hands in his lap.

"We'll need witnesses," he said.

"Lisa."

"Will you be able to handle that, knowing what you know now?"

"She's both my best friend and my sister. She's the only one I want to stand up with me. How about you? Chance?"

"Yeah."

She took a deep breath. "Our parents."

He shook his head.

"We can't not invite them, Ted. If I were a parent, I

would be so hurt not to be invited to my child's wedding. It'll be their choice. They can say no, but we can't leave them out. What kind of beginning to our marriage would that be? Your parents would blame me for denying them the chance to see their only child get married. My mom would blame you. It could take a long time to soothe those particular hurt feelings. At the very least we have to tell them before it happens, not after."

He thought it over, saw the hopeful look in her eyes. "My parents are in Toronto."

"I can't believe you're making excuses. That suggests to me that you do think they'll object to—"

"No. I don't, Sara Beth. I just want to get married without making a big production of it."

"I wouldn't call this wedding a big production."

She was right. "Okay, I do see your point. So, it looks like we have a lot of phone calls to make." He touched her hair. "Are you upset about not having the big, white wedding? Is it something you've dreamed about?"

"Maybe a little, but that was a girlhood fantasy. The reality is just fine."

"You are one incredible woman," he said.

She smiled and kissed him. "Don't you forget it."

It was the strangest, most wonderful whirlwind of Sara Beth's life, full of joy and surprises. First came the phone calls to Boston. Lisa whooped so loudly that Sara Beth had to pull the phone away from her ear. It was so hard not to blurt out that they were sisters, but Sara Beth had talked it over with Ted and decided to keep it to herself for now. Maybe the right time would come, but it wasn't today.

Chance came next but he'd been called in for a difficult delivery of triplets, plus he had no one to cover for him. He was disappointed that he couldn't attend, but promised to throw Ted a postwedding bachelor party.

Sara Beth called her mother next, inviting her to join them at the airport, to fly to the wedding, to be part of it. Sara Beth had held her breath, waiting for a question or an "Are you sure?" It never came. She said she'd be there with bells on.

Ted hadn't called his parents in front of her, and all he said was they'd try to make it. Sara Beth wanted to delay the event until they could, but Ted slowly shook his head.

Sara Beth refused to be hurt for herself, but she was sorry for Ted.

Ted's friend Rourke Devlin insisted on coming along and being the best man. When he climbed onto the plane, *his* plane, Sara Beth recognized him, remembered seeing him at Shots with Ted and Chance, solving that mystery. Then a new intrigue began as Rourke and Lisa made eye contact and went still for a few seconds. Lisa glanced away first, but Sara Beth caught them sneaking looks at each other the whole flight to Las Vegas.

It didn't matter that their flight landed in the middle of the night. The city was lit and teeming with tourists. They checked into the Bellagio, had something to eat, got a few hours of sleep, then Sara Beth, her mother and Lisa shopped for a wedding dress, finding a stunning white sheath scattered with a few beads to give it sparkle.

She felt beautiful.

At high noon, she linked her arm through her mother's and moved to the top of the aisle, ready to marry the man she loved, who looked at her with such love in return that it stopped her stomach from churning.

Then she saw his parents sitting in the front row, and joy filled her, warm and satisfying, completing her beautiful day. They stood, were smiling at her, as was Ted, who'd changed his tie to one she'd bought him covered with teddy bears. She carried the bouquet he'd given her in New York.

The processional music started. Lisa gave her a thumbs-up. Rourke cupped Ted's shoulder and said something that made him smile. Holding hands, Ted's parents eyed him as Sara Beth and her mother came down the aisle, Ted smiling at her. She beamed back.

He was right. Whether or not she was pregnant, this was good—perfect, in fact.

The ceremony was short but memorable, their I-dos followed by a kiss she would always remember. They didn't walk back up the aisle but greeted everyone where they stood. Got hugs from Lisa and Grace. Congratulations from Rourke.

Then Ted's parents approached.

Penny took Sara Beth's hand. "All his life, I've been wondering who he would choose, hoping he would find his soul mate, as I did mine. You make him happy. I've never heard him sound so carefree, and he's obviously so much in love. Thank you for bringing that to him." She kissed Sara Beth's cheek.

"Thank you," Sara Beth whispered, close to tears. "He's truly a gift in my life."

"Sara Beth," Brant Bonner said.

She waited, not expecting anything but kind words now. Still her pulse pounded in her ears as she waited for what he had to say.

"I know I didn't have the privilege of watching you grow up, like I did my son. I'll bet you were a beautiful, mischievous child." He smiled and looked to Grace for confirmation, receiving it in a nod and return smile.

"I know you didn't have a father around to make your life easier in ways that fathers can. But I want you to know that I'd be honored if you called me Dad."

Tears started to fall from Sara Beth's eyes, blurring her vision. "Thank you. Yes, I'd like to do that. Dad."

Everyone laughed a little shakily, then Brant pulled something from behind his back, a soft brown teddy bear with a red heart sewn on its chest. "Welcome to the family, daughter."

Sara Beth reached for it, this amazing symbol, such a small thing to bind people together. "You told him how much I ached for a father," she said to Ted, brushing at her tears. "About the teddy bear."

"Yes. And I won't apologize—" Ted emphasized.

She put a hand to his mouth, stopping the words. "No one's ever done what you've done—anything so kind, so thoughtful, *so loving* for me—and that's saying a lot, Ted, because I have a lot of great friends, and a wonderful mother."

Their guests had walked away, giving them a moment. "I am the luckiest woman alive. I love you so much." She went up on tiptoe to kiss him.

And the absentminded scientist gave her his single-minded attention, a silent promise that she would always come first.

* * * * *

*Don't miss the next chapter in the new
Special Edition continuity,*
THE BABY CHASE.
*When waitress Jenny Labeaux is invited to a
charity ball by playboy doctor Chance Demetrios,
she knows their attraction is too good to be true.
Little does she know that Chance is finally ready
to settle down—and Jenny and her little girl might
just be the family he's always wanted!
Don't miss*
CINDERELLA AND THE PLAYBOY
*By Lois Faye Dyer
On sale April 2010,
wherever Silhouette books are sold.*

Harlequin offers a romance for every mood!
See below for a sneak peek from our paranormal
romance line, Silhouette® Nocturne™.
Enjoy a preview of REUNION by USA TODAY best-
selling author Lindsay McKenna.

Aella closed her eyes and sensed a distinct shift, like
movement from the world around her to the unseen world.

She opened her eyes. And had a slight shock at the
man standing ten feet away. He wasn't just any man. Her
heart leaped and pounded. He reminded her of a fierce
warrior from an ancient civilization. Incan? She wasn't
sure but she felt his deep power and masculinity.

I'm Aella. Are you the guardian of this sacred site?
she asked, hoping her telepathy was strong.

Fox's entire body soared with joy. Fox struggled to
put his personal pleasure aside.

Greetings, Aella. I'm the assistant guardian to this
sacred area. You may call me Fox. How can I be of
service to you, Aella? he asked.

I'm searching for a green sphere. A legend says that
the Emperor Pachacuti had seven emerald spheres
created for the Emerald Key necklace. He had seven of
his priestesses and priests travel the world to hide these
spheres from evil forces. It is said that when all seven
spheres are found, restrung and worn, that Light will
return to the Earth. The fourth sphere is here, at your

sacred site. Are you aware of it? Aella held her breath. She loved looking at him, especially his sensual mouth. The desire to kiss him came out of nowhere.

Fox was stunned by the request. *I know of the Emerald Key necklace because I served the emperor at the time it was created. However, I did not realize that one of the spheres is here.*

Aella felt sad. Why? Every time she looked at Fox, her heart felt as if it would tear out of her chest. *May I stay in touch with you as I work with this site?* she asked.

Of course. Fox wanted nothing more than to be here with her. To absorb her ephemeral beauty and hear her speak once more.

Aella's spirit lifted. What *was* this strange connection between them? Her curiosity was strong, but she had more pressing matters. In the next few days, Aella knew her life would change forever. How, she had no idea....

Look for REUNION
by USA TODAY bestselling author
Lindsay McKenna,
available April 2010, only from
Silhouette® Nocturne™.

HARLEQUIN®

INTRIGUE®

WILL THIS REUNITED FAMILY
BE STRONG ENOUGH TO EXPOSE
A LURKING KILLER?

FIND OUT IN THIS ALL-NEW
THRILLING TRILOGY FROM TOP
HARLEQUIN INTRIGUE AUTHOR

B.J. DANIELS

WHITEHORSE
MONTANA

Winchester Ranch

GUN-SHY BRIDE—*April 2010*

HITCHED—*May 2010*

TWELVE-GAUGE GUARDIAN—
June 2010

ROMANCE, RIVALRY
AND A FAMILY REUNITED

THE BRIDES
of
BELLA ROSA

William Valentine and his beloved wife, Lucia, live
a beautiful life together, but when his former love Rosa
and the secret family they had together resurface,
an instant rivalry is formed. Can these families
get through the past and come together as one?

———————

Step into the world of Bella Rosa
beginning this April with

Beauty and the Reclusive Prince
by
RAYE MORGAN

Eight volumes to collect and treasure!

www.eHarlequin.com

HR17650

HARLEQUIN *Presents*

2 Stories in 1

HER MEDITERRANEAN PLAYBOY

Sexy and dangerous—he wants you in his bed!

The sky is blue, the azure sea is crashing
against the golden sand and the sun is hot.

The conditions are perfect for
a scorching Mediterranean seduction
from two irresistible untamed playboys!

Indulge your senses with these two delicious stories

A MISTRESS AT THE ITALIAN'S COMMAND
by *Melanie Milburne*

ITALIAN BOSS, HOUSEKEEPER MISTRESS
by *Kate Hewitt*

Available April 2010 from Harlequin Presents!

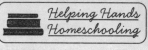

REQUEST YOUR FREE BOOKS!

2 FREE NOVELS PLUS 2 FREE GIFTS!

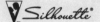

SPECIAL EDITION

Life, Love and Family!

YES! Please send me 2 FREE Silhouette® Special Edition® novels and my 2 FREE gifts (gifts are worth about $10). After receiving them, if I don't wish to receive any more books, I can return the shipping statement marked "cancel." If I don't cancel, I will receive 6 brand-new novels every month and be billed just $4.24 per book in the U.S. or $4.99 per book in Canada. That's a saving of 15% off the cover price! It's quite a bargain! Shipping and handling is just 50¢ per book in the U.S. and 75¢ per book in Canada.* I understand that accepting the 2 free books and gifts places me under no obligation to buy anything. I can always return a shipment and cancel at any time. Even if I never buy another book from Silhouette, the two free books and gifts are mine to keep forever.

235 SDN E4NC   335 SDN E4NN

Name _____ (PLEASE PRINT)

Address _____ Apt. #

City _____ State/Prov. _____ Zip/Postal Code

Signature (if under 18, a parent or guardian must sign)

Mail to the **Silhouette Reader Service:**
IN U.S.A.: P.O. Box 1867, Buffalo, NY 14240-1867
IN CANADA: P.O. Box 609, Fort Erie, Ontario L2A 5X3

Not valid for current subscribers to Silhouette Special Edition books.

Want to try two free books from another line?
Call 1-800-873-8635 or visit www.morefreebooks.com.

* Terms and prices subject to change without notice. Prices do not include applicable taxes. N.Y. residents add applicable sales tax. Canadian residents will be charged applicable provincial taxes and GST. Offer not valid in Quebec. This offer is limited to one order per household. All orders subject to approval. Credit or debit balances in a customer's account(s) may be offset by any other outstanding balance owed by or to the customer. Please allow 4 to 6 weeks for delivery. Offer available while quantities last.

Your Privacy: Silhouette is committed to protecting your privacy. Our Privacy Policy is available online at www.eHarlequin.com or upon request from the Reader Service. From time to time we make our lists of customers available to reputable third parties who may have a product or service of interest to you. If you would prefer we not share your name and address, please check here. ☐

Help us get it right—We strive for accurate, respectful and relevant communications. To clarify or modify your communication preferences, visit us at www.ReaderService.com/consumerchoice.

SSE10